Unterm Neomond

UNDER THE NEOMOON

Wolfgang Hilbig

Translated from German by
Isabel Fargo Cole

TWO LINES
PRESS

Originally published in German as *Unterm Neomond. Erzählungen* by Wolfgang Hilbig
Copyright © 1982, S. Fischer Verlag GmbH, Frankfurt am Main
Translation © 2024 by Isabel Fargo Cole

Two Lines Press
582 Market Street, Suite 700, San Francisco, CA 94104
www.twolinespress.com

ISBN: 978-1-949641-61-5
Ebook ISBN: 978-1-949641-62-2

Cover design by Andrew Walters
Typeset by Wengrow
Printed in the United States of America

Library of Congress Cataloging-in-Publication Data

Names: Hilbig, Wolfgang, 1941-2007, author. | Cole, Isabel Fargo, 1973-
translator.
Title: Under the neomoon / Wolfgang Hilbig ; translated from German by
Isabel Fargo Cole.
Other titles: Unterm Neomond. English
Description: San Francisco, CA : Two Lines Press, 2024. | Summary: "In
these early prose writings, Wolfgang Hilbig (1941-2007) summons menac-
ing visions of smoldering factory pits, rampant nature, and split identities"--
Provided by publisher.
Identifiers: LCCN 2023056115 (print) | LCCN 2023056116 (ebook) |
ISBN 9781949641615 (paperback) | ISBN 9781949641622 (ebook)
Subjects: LCGFT: Short stories.
Classification: LCC PT2668.I323 U5813 2024 (print) | LCC PT2668.
I323 (ebook) | DDC 833/.914--dc23/eng/20231211
LC record available at https://lccn.loc.gov/2023056115
LC ebook record available at https://lccn.loc.gov/2023056116

This publication is supported in part by an award from the National
Endowment for the Arts. The translation of this book was supported by a
grant from the Goethe-Institut.

Also by Wolfgang Hilbig
Available from Two Lines Press

THE SLEEP OF THE RIGHTEOUS

OLD RENDERING PLANT

THE TIDINGS OF THE TREES

THE FEMALES

THE INTERIM

CONTENTS

I

II

III

I

BREAKING LOOSE

It was summer, and all summer long, there were days when I fretted at being late out of bed, late to put my shirt and pants on, late to leave the house, so late that it barely refreshed me, but why should it, the morning chased away my weariness every day when it wasn't yet too late, so late that I'd wearied by the time it drew toward noon again, and it seemed to go too slowly for me, walking down my path. At the end of the path I reached an old dead canal arm that beckoned me onward, but maybe I never did reach it, because I was walking forever, all summer, sometimes too slow, sometimes so fast that I broke out in sweat when I lingered in spots that the sun struck with full force, and even at a brisk walk I felt the ground grow hot in this summer, I felt it in the burning of my bare soles standing on the scarce stones grown hot on the firm-trodden ground. But did I really linger, didn't I hurry onward, day after day, each time I faltered in the middle of the path as though I'd forgotten something. O misfortune, O ill humor, how oh-so-sure was I of my remaining, of my silence, of the beckoning of that old canal arm, ground broken years ago. Ah, did I really linger in that hot place near what I called the house, sometimes inside that abode when I never left the house, sometimes in the grass, prodigious in its growth, and sometimes on the clay bank, dry and fissured, hard as glass shards, down below, where the water line had fallen. Often enough there was nothing I lacked, but often enough certain things seemed forgotten, but no, often enough I lacked for nothing, when my forgetfulness grew prodigiously. Sometimes, ah, all too often, I had to take a rest, the haste, the hustle flickered in my veins, the grass and the thickets that I called riotous, that line my path and incubate their shadows where the dew lasts till noon, till at noon the heat sinks down and in its vapor the riotous reaches of the wild cherry trees loom over me, an imagined vapor that shuts my eyes when I doze off, fatigued and drenched and sleepy in this green vapor of the hot dew that had long oppressed me. Whenever I'm here, and I'm here all summer long, I'm enticed by those thickets, I ought to plunge in, sleep, and forget what I might be lacking, the things I might need on my way, a hundred yards long. I lacked for nothing, and I couldn't wait, when I hurried onward, cajoling myself in unfinished sentences and devouring my breath, couldn't wait for the next day, when it was morning, not noon, to tell myself, today, why not today, go tranquil and good-humored down to the boat, then down the canal, then out on the lake, and never have to turn around. But whenever I lingered, still buoyant, as though it were early in the morning, the dew and the thickets resisted my haste, before I was fully asleep it was noon, when I woke I thought it was evening, each time I beheld, then forgot, my prosperity in the fading light, and enfeebled and weary, weary of my wrath and weary of my malice, weary of my misfortune, I plunged down on the ground to rest, and on I went, all night long, vowing not to be idle, not to linger, not to forget. Still dreaming I started out, having barely dozed off I reached the canal bank, saw the boat on the bank, saw that it had sprung a leak, its planks dried and rotted long ago. And I beheld my prosperity in the nocturnal light, and vowed to set fire to the shack where I lived, in the morning, once I was rid of my weariness, fire to free myself from the alcohol of this summer and the books I'd brought with me, fire, once I'd recovered, kindling the bed and the books I no longer read, fire kindling my prosperity's clothes closet, fire transforming the planks of my walls and furniture into thickets of fire. But in the morning, when I woke, I was too tired, or I'd forgotten. Before coming here, I'd wearied of a prosperity where hulking old married women leaned out their windows in the morning waiting for the postwoman, I hated being where I was when it was summer, summer when the refrigerators wound themselves up, regular as automatic clocks, incensing me, and when the feather beds draped over the windowsills made shapes I admired, and when the bogus carpets were beaten in the yards until the noise incensed me. Ah, no. I wanted to leave, to come here, I wanted to go in rags from sheer grief. I barely remember, it was as though my grief incensed me so much that I made everything into money, as much money as possible, grabbing it and hiding it on my person, so much that I took my books and came here, where I pondered, and waited to feel better to start out across the lake. Have I forgotten something. Ah, here, all this summer, there are days I wake up thinking: now, this very morning, this day or never, this very summer. Until I decide it's too soon, or too late, until the sun, weariness, ignorance assails me. And I had a great yearning for a different prosperity, for the mild climate of other shores I still saw in my sleep, just as I'd known them, the snow-white houses of Obereselsrück, Canaan's green hills covered with peppermint, and in front of them, behind them, plains veined by tranquil rivers, have I forgotten something, a great yearning for money, for slow books with no plot, for gray skies, for skies raining down on cattle herds. No, I wanted to stop talking, to start being silent, but I forgot, yes, I wanted to bark and howl like a dog, grunt and sing like a hippopotamus, but linger no longer in this eloquent wasteland. It's a thicket that molders and collapses in the fall, that shoots up from the mud in spring, I call it riotous. It's that crippling truncated canal, ground broken, started and broken off years ago, left in the lurch by its dredgers, allegory of all unfinished work, allegory of all broken starts, dead-ended in a thicket of work, its mounds of clay and gravel that refuse to find a home here, the subterranean soil, pierced by young grass and prodigiously laid waste to. By this dwindling water in which my boat is rotting. Have I forgotten something. I'm so sure of my remaining, of my silence here, that I never begin it. I have forgotten, it smells of our origin. Of rushes, it smells of origin and birth beneath this out-gushing sun, it smells of origin, of alcoholic summer, of birth and return through that hot place in my sleep. If I woke up at last, I'd find my way down, the boat would still carry me, I'd forget to return, I'd break out, leave everything here behind to escape.

BUNGALOWS

Bungalows, that's what they call these shabby cabins made of timber-framed pressboard painted green, standing behind the inn, next to the forest. A coworker who's usually away shares one of these cabins with me; the rest are empty; at the end of the summer most of the staff decamped to the city, so I'm almost always alone here. What's there to do after dinner, when I always end up eating too much; I go outside, melancholy body heavy as stone, cigarette clamped between my lips, down the sandy path around the inn through the garden to the lake, and out on the dock to gaze into the fog and the dark. It's dark by seven, over the water the air is brisk, but still not too chilly for me, I'm used to the cool evenings. There's no wind, the shadow of a small boat lies rigid by the dock, the sky holds just a few stars, a hint of the moon somewhere, ahead of me I can't see far, fog towers inert over the motionless black water.

O what a fall this is. From the lit window in the inn's top floor, laughter drifts into the garden, the same as every evening there's a party going on. It doesn't bother me,

11

I've got no cause to go up there. Still, I turn to look back through the garden, empty but for the mighty chestnut trees, garden chairs and tables long since stowed away; a ray of light slips out the window, lost in the crowns of the chestnuts looming in front, black with gleaming edges; there's just a faint light in the garden, but I see the leaves falling slowly from the trees.

O what a fall, even the days in the still-warm sun grow foggier the earlier the afternoons end, cottony white vapor rises from the water; these afternoons there are hardly any guests, even now all they see is bleakness, the winter bleakness of this place, and I idle away the afternoons, waiting for the evenings when panic approaches. In the winter this will be a place of icy cold, the city far away; by then I hope to have ended my feud with the couple who run the inn and escaped back to the city. By day I go barefoot, a good feeling in the cool sand; after dark, flimsy rubber sandals protect my feet from the dry chestnut husks that lie around in masses, I hear my sandals rustle in the leaves, the yellow leaves that fall in the daytime faster and faster, in the daytime when the sun still shines but the fogs grow more dogged; in the hours of light the lake is bright blue, with flocks of black ducks floating on the water by the rushes. But now it's dark.

Bungalows. I remember all the stories I used to read about hunters and explorers in Africa. With ink drawings. The bungalows in those drawings would be standing at the edge of the primeval forest, flat roofs jutting over open verandas, longish buildings, whitewashed, with sturdy wooden shutters, verandas propped, in the manner of stilt dwellings, on thick wooden piles, the inhabitants posing in front in their pith helmets, self-assured in their ludicrous knee-length trousers, pale thin legs in tall laced boots, cartridge belts around their waists, often brandishing firearms. But the black natives were well built, naked gleaming bodies, their bearing deferential, but secretly contemptuous, straight from the primeval forest, resembling, in their multitudes, in their bewildering, unpredictable incursions, some unknown, dangerous vegetation. But the whites knew how to defend their bungalows, with firearms, there were stories where throngs of black forms suddenly emerged at night from the forest, swinging long spears with broad spearheads, masses of black forms all around the bungalow, suddenly breaking out in shrill ululations, barely held back by the feeble rifle fire.

My bungalow here can't be compared with those. This here is a pathless region, the passenger boats that dock a few times a day in summer are the only way to reach the inn the bungalows belong to; it lies in a lonely, picturesquely wild spot at the lake's end, and the city is far away. Somewhere on an island in the lake archaeologists are said to have found traces of an infinitely distant era, even a carved wooden idol. The Huns, wild warrior hordes from the far reaches of Asia, are said to have reached this region on their devastating raids, murdering and looting under the legendary King Atilla. I don't know if these stories are true. One time I saw how an illustrator drew the Huns. Shiny shaved skulls with black beards, Asiatic eyes that the artist gave a glowering, furtive look, fists clutching curved, razor-sharp weapons.

This region here is for the most part pathless. I know how the forest looks from seeing it by day; it begins just behind the bungalows, bounded toward the beach by a fence, collapsed in places, with "no trespassing" signs. At first it's light and open, with sparse underbrush between trees that can barely stand upright on the wet ground, tall grass, no paths, huge toppled trees everywhere, dead and stripped of bark, the ground is swampy, swamp everywhere, a black morass, vast dully glinting pools all around, and soon the woods grow denser, wild and snarled, impenetrable thickets, tall dark-green water grasses, no animals, just birds, and the ground is swamp, wet, deep, black swamp. There is no path through this forest, there never was, why should there be, when past this forest comes an eternity of more forest, swamp, water, on and on for equally pathless, unknown expanses.

But what if there are secret paths. Trails only they know, and not another soul, because they were already here centuries ago. And this bungalow, this fragile cabin where I don't have a rifle. And if I did, I'm sure it would be no use against their curved, sharp weapons. Besides, I won't see them, paralyzed by fear, until they loom in my doorway at night. They come noiselessly, crouching, down the secret paths, single file, their ranks are endless, they come from all directions, not a twig snaps beneath their soles, they know the tracks through the swamp. And at the same time they're sure to come across the lake, countless fires emerging from the fog, those are their slender canoes, each with a torch at its prow. They're coming from that island somewhere in the lake, from all the wooded shores, they've reached the beach now, they're dousing their torches and coming, my heavy body feels them coming. I haven't caught a glimpse of them. They come unglimpsed and noiseless, from the woods, across the lake, from all sides. Maybe those stories are true, they exist, and they're coming, I don't know.

IDYLL

Under the trees grew such enticing grass. For an hour now I'd been fuming at my light-colored suit, my white shirt, and worse still was my rage at the jam-packed bag I had to haul. A horse-drawn wagon, dawdling as the heat set in, had taken me a stretch, and the driver had recommended, as the shortest way to town, a path that led away from the main road; I'd set out at the crack of dawn, in town new rooms awaited me. Now I reckoned it was eight o'clock, a September morning under the sun's spell. It was a northerly region, the country flat as a tabletop, and contrary to expectations, the summers in this area seemed especially long-lasting, from early May to late September summer reigned in the woods. My path took me through meadows where trees stood, not too closely, but I couldn't see far ahead. It was already turning hot, my newly purchased shoes had a coat of pale dust, my feet smarted in the stiff leather; it struck me that the grass by the wayside must still be cool and fresh, never in my thirty years had I really lain in the grass, what a fateful omission, what malicious circumstances had barred me from savoring that blessing. That sprawl in the grass, that utter submission to the weightless murmur filtering through the eardrums, through the closed lids into the perturbed brain—that must have been it, the thing I was deprived of, a mute curse eluding consciousness, suspended over my life at all times. I kept on walking, since early morning with my free hand I'd been smoking cigarette after cigarette, the nicotine burned on my tongue and phlegm clogged my mouth, toxic in its bitterness; I'd gotten up too early, but my body was barely tired yet, my nerves were tired, something like a semi-anesthesia was lodged in my head. Before I actually lay down, the trees ahead grew denser, I heard a rushing noise, as though ahead of me water were rushing, a tall hedge of underbrush rose suddenly between the trees, leaving a tiny gap for my path, now just a beaten track, to slip through. Behind the hedge, once I'd passed through it, I saw a broad brook, dammed by a weir, the water plunged rushing over the weir and took the form of a noise suspended over the surroundings like an invisible cloud of water dust. I had to accustom myself to that rushing to hear the morning's other sounds over it once more. Along the weir a wooden bridge led across the watercourse into a big overgrown garden or rather a sort of orchard that seemed to have gone long uncared-for. The branches of the trees grew snarled and unpruned, the unharvested fruits had fallen to rot in the grass, swarming with wasps, bushes and weeds shot up beneath the trees all around, the whole garden seemed suffused by the scent of old honey. — Once I'd crossed the bridge, I saw an old mill a bit farther down the brook, its gigantic paddlewheel rising two-thirds of the way from the water. The wheel stood still, and drawing nearer I saw that the wood was black, water-logged, rotten, the paddles broken, at the waterline the wood was green from algae, while the upper portion was bleaching out, turning white again in the sun. The mill was uninhabited, the doors torn from their frames, streaks of sun crossed the floors of the halls, covered with shards and debris. Outside, woodbine seemed to hold up the old half-timbered walls, washing like a green wave over the building, growing almost to the roof and into the broken windows. — It's hot, I said, this is a mill. A deserted mill. — My thoughts were shockingly banal, perhaps, but they didn't shock me. My head seemed impervious, completely closed, I had to repeat myself: This is a mill, it's deserted. — In the rooms, apart from a rickety table, a broken chair, the debris of a caved-in tile stove, apart from tattered curtain remnants and newspaper scraps on the floorboards, nothing more was left; someone had defecated in the corner; the cellar stairs probably led to the former workroom, but I didn't trust them to carry my weight; cautiously I climbed the wooden steps to the top floor, in whose rooms I found the same grimy vacancy. Now the rooms and corridors were pervaded by a twilight suggesting the warmth outside, the white sunlight spilling across the roof, the meadows, the brook. Looking out the top-floor window, I saw that the green water had taken on a blinding, shimmering hue, throwing back a spray of sunlight, reflections playing and flaring in the vines that ran riot right next to my head. Returning to the ground floor, I found it twilit and cool, only the small windows let rectangular sunbeams slant to the floor; it was the thick dust that seemed to keep the air so cool here, a dust that covered everything, older-seeming than the dust on my shoes. Suddenly I felt that if I daubed the dust on the tabletop with my finger and tasted it, I'd have the familiar taste of the floury crust of a loaf on my tongue. Stepping back outside, I realized that I was thirsty. — I want a drink of water, I thought, and then I really was walking down the low bank to the brook and bending down to the water. Here the current was almost imperceptible, I saw it dark and pure, too deep to make out the bottom. I scooped up water and drank, it was cold and tasted faintly of algae. I rinsed the nicotine taste from my mouth and spat into the water, saw that flurry drift slowly away, leaving my reflection, hunkered there in the light-colored suit, the end of the red tie dangling in the water. Annoyed, I leaped back up the bank, where my bag stood; I felt tempted to kick it into the water. But then I thought it would be more sensible to take out a short-sleeved shirt and a pair of light linen pants beforehand. — That's my first sensible thought today, I said; everything I thought was so infinitely banal, so unsatisfying, and yet I had to think it. — After that I can toss the bag in the water. Toss the bag in the water, I said, I said it as though I were learning to talk, the bag in the water, with my shoes inside, with my suit and tie. Let that baggage float away, down the brooks, down the rivers, for all I care, all the way to the Vistula, all the way to the Danube, all the way to the oceans. — Wearily I picked up the bag again, turned away from the mill and started back, slowly, keeping to the brook. — I've always wanted a mill, rooms in a mill, I thought, and yet I'm walking slowly away. Slowly, but still. — I said to myself: it's got to stop, the state my mind's in, the only thoughts that won't perturb me are spiteful, wrathful thoughts, those are the best thoughts to have. Spiteful, destructive thoughts. The devil take it, there's no cause for them, not today, not here and not in the country I live in. — But I forgot things so quickly, maybe I'd forgotten the reason for my spiteful thoughts, what was it that let me forget so quickly, I searched my benumbed mind and found that all the reasons for my wrath had vanished; what was it in this country—the gas of the sun, the gas of peace, the vapor of the stillness that was decaying and working away here by that decaying mill—that drowned my invigorating wrath in this tranquil concord of water and sun. — You ought to take a rest, I thought, but change your clothes first, it won't do to lie in the grass in this light-colored suit. — But already I was tossing aside the bag and sprawling out. The grass was pleasantly warm and damp, the sun shone in my eyes, and blinking, already nearly insensate, I felt sleep draw near. — Let the devil go into town, I thought, let the devil go calm down in the security of town. — I was calmed by that thought, my need for sleep was so strong, my body featherlight, I knew I was really already sleeping, yet I could rise at any moment and go back to the mill, my feet just grazing the tips of the grass, borne by sun-warmth and sleep, and before that sleep deepened I argued: what am I supposed to do in town, hunkered in my rooms, paying rent, paying taxes, gobbling food, guzzling drink, living like other people, forgetting, spending all my time forgetting, sitting in my chair forgetting, staring out the window at the forgotten street, until I can hardly get up from my forgotten chair to strangle myself with my necktie. Am I supposed to get to know people there, people whose friendliness sickens me. Am I supposed to work there, work, work, work. How dreary, how pathetic to work. How degraded to get haircuts, to shave, how miserable to wash and dress according to the fashion. How sad to be healthy and sound, placid, forgetful, how tiresome, how tiresome to know what country I live in, and know it without wrath, and have to hold this always and without wrath in my dreary consciousness. —

And already within this sleep I stand up, ramble over to the mill, step into its rooms damp and dirty, unkempt and wild.

Hey maid of the mill, I shout as I enter the hall, everything's provided for. See this bottle of brandy clenched in my fist, I haven't forgotten a thing. Hurry and slice one of those sweet, flour-dusted breads of yours. All summer long you'll have no need to hold me here. And in the winter evenings, when the house resounds with our laughter, we'll find out what I'm good for. Then I'll go and chop wood until the smoke of our fire rises for all to see, with all its might from the ancient chimney.

THIRST

In the evenings, in the summer twilight, with a southwest breeze blowing, all the town's streets fill with the cloying, unendurable smell of cadavers.

Everywhere windows are slammed shut, the few lone pedestrians withdraw into the crowded, hermetically shut pubs. Everyone knows it's the fumes from a factory on the outskirts that produces some sort of ingredients for detergents, where masses of cadavers, animal cadavers, are rendered and work begins at nightfall.

But none of the drinkers in the pubs know when the smell in the streets will lift, in their barrooms, too, the windows and doors are slammed shut, curtains are drawn, you settle in as though resolved to drink till the early daybreak, you shun the streets as though dreading an epidemic, you sit and drink in the awareness of a smell outside the doors, a smell casting, as a blue gas, a dull phosphor glow through the night, you think you hear it gnawing at the houses' outer skins, you think you hear desiccation spreading inward through the wood of the doorframes, you must drown this awareness within you.

You must drink until all memory of that repulsive gas yields to a drunken, reeling flood of thoughts that revolve around the barroom's increasingly inscrutable goings-on. Yellow and green are the hues of all things capable of warding off the pestilence. At the counter of yellow wood, fogged by dampness, about to vanish behind swaths of stale breath and tobacco smoke, beer's being poured in an endless series of glasses that race off to the tables, the tablecloths are swept to the floor, and on the wet wood the glasses slide faster into the splayed hands, lots and lots of yellow foam-crowned glasses that soon seem to merge, so that all at once you see them as a single wave of cool-bitter, white-yellow beer foam surging toward you, but still so shallow that it fails to reach your round, open mouth; it reaches waist-high, and from every opening, every sucking, protruding orifice, every hose-end, the unconsumed dregs flow back, trickling away in quick loops on the floorboards; the voices in the room have the raucous force of a storm, resounding in the breasts of the people around you, though their gaping mouths seem to release no sound. Meanwhile, the thirst grows more pressing, more unstillable, as—taking material form, mutely announcing its yearning—it drips and runs from all the bodies; the open mouths' cavities are tinged green, are sponges, displaying in panic the threat of desiccation; even as the heads' clarities yield to a frothing, spurting, streaming confusion, even as the eyes turn to fungi, the yellow shape of the bar counter looms like a rock in the fog, and the second wave rolls in from there, breaking at neck level, wetting your hair for the first time, but still you haven't gotten your share; you stand up, nearly toppling onto your outstretched arms, you try to drag your disintegrating body to the front, to the yellow light of the bar, for your thirst is uncontrollable, gigantic, infernal, but the third wave hurls you back, you go under; as through a soft, flexible channel with all the floodgates unlocked, the liquid floods you without cease, falling over backward, you feel your thirst turn grotesque and ridiculous; when your limbs begin to drift away you feel the green and idiotic thirst of a creature that dwells in liquid, a thirst that persists independent of all satiation. The mouths of the people around you have stretched to foaming flews, swollen to shaggy trunks, lengthened to amphibious bills, all the bodies are a glistening green, covered with silver scales, all the limbs are strong and supple, equipped with splayed webs, dangling fins, fishtails, rhythmically vibrating gills, they're all diving, swimming, gliding creatures, releasing streams of bubbles and touching each other with gaping snouts; it's awful to see their obscene pleasure as they roll over on their backs at the level of the dim lamps and, inert for a time, a mere snuffling their only sign of life, press white-yellow glistening belly against belly. You watch with horror, speechless and already remote from humanity, hung with dripping heavy pelts, gurgling as you struggle for breath, surrounded by the grunting of Tritons and the tittering of Nereids, assaulted by the lust of great foam-sucking cockles, ogled, with crabby, stinging cnidarian tentacles already twitching around your loins and thighs, instinctively almost at home in a world of damp and fogs, almost submerged in the true monsters' deeps, yet still senselessly thirsty; but at last, long past curfew, the full horror dawning on you, you jump up, reeling, and fling up your arms to scream, to create, through your screams, room for the human breast, but already you feel your arm seized; you're grabbed and drawn into a sleepy, swaying circle and included in a stately chant intoned as ebb and flow, pouring from mouth to mouth like sluggish currents of heavier water.

If, at this hour—the air fresh again, the southwester having long since chased the smell of rot from town—a traveler hastening through streets swept empty should glimpse light in the window of a pub, and knock repeatedly for admittance, urgently but in vain, puzzled at first, then shouting out an angry curse: A plague upon this town… his ear, inclined in alarm toward the pane, would be answered by a ponderous song taking form from a din, seeming explanation as well as threat, but always so indistinct that both are intuited rather than grasped:

> We know full well, we know full well
> then and now in the fires of hell
> they burned the bones, they burned the pelts.
> If you're wise you'll sell the cow
> sell the dog and sell the sow
> sell the goat to Ponikau
> the cash will quench the thirst of hell.

Horror shooting through every limb, the traveler forgets his thirst. Native to an ever-fragrant region, from an era following the Flood in which all creatures have been assigned to their proper species, and land and sea divided, he takes this for a town in the sway of wild beasts, beasts interbreeding in the ritual light of mingled yellow-blue sacrificial fires to produce the most horrid monsters, ah, he'd count himself lucky to spend the rest of the night in the fields, to flee before the club-brandishing cattle drivers burst out through all the doors; he sees the silent houses lurking in the first morning light; he'd prefer the stench of a stable on the fields' edge.

THE END OF THE NIGHT

Old story, just before midnight, the clattering stagecoach
nears—more dragged than drawn by the panting horses,
the lash dancing about their sweat-drenched flanks having driven the beasts to a pace unconscionable on the
miserable mud-covered roads—and on the sludgy pond
of a village square the coach comes to a standstill like
a roar falling silent. The traveling gentleman steps out,
heedlessly tramping through the puddles in his boots,
clearly in great haste, yet before turning to the inn he
gazes at the sky. Prodigious black backward-looking
clouds drift menacingly low, the village square, without
a single light, is filled with cold wind, rain is imminent;
the horses had barely halted when the coachman dozed
off, slumped over on the coachbox. The inn door is locked,
the windows armored with stout wooden shutters. The
letters on the sign above the door are illegible; the gentleman sets down his little leather case in the doorway
and pounds on one shutter with a gloved fist, but there
is no reply. — Never, at this hour, would he dare to cry:
Open up, open up, give me a bed for just this half a night,

it's almost midnight, the horses are exhausted, why, I was announced, and tomorrow I'm expected in the city, yes, I'm the long-awaited one, my bag is filled with ducats... no one would hear him. The gentleman puts his ear to the shutter, hammers at the wood with both fists, he hears the blows resound through the house, the empty house, no doors shut off the inner rooms and hold out the racket, they've been torn down, broken from the walls, no furniture in the abandoned house, the floors covered with rubble, the stairs caved in, the front door boarded up. Seized by icy pain, the gentleman hears the echo of his blows die away; as he looks back imploringly at the coachman, the clouds part, for one moment a moonbeam strikes the figure whose boldly outstretched arm rests on the rail of the coachbox; from the wide sleeve, clear to see, dangle the snow-white fingers of a skeletal hand. Never would the gentleman dare address that coachman, mindful of the grisly skull hidden by the dark hat. As the darkness returns, and the rain sets in, the gentleman feels his wet face, and abandoning all hope he thinks: Soon the last night of the old era will end, and the new...I'll never reach it, although I was announced. And watching the plundered houses of this village recede, I'll be left with my cold knowledge in this dying world, oh, knowing that I fell a few human words short of a goal I pursued for a century, knowing that the ears of those to come would profit from certain words of mine. But now the light to come will blaze with flowing blood, for their ears shall be cut off, their limbs broken, their hearts torn asunder, their bodies shall be burned to ash, and streets paved with ash shall take into the fire the bodies of those to come... and grasping this I see that the horses will never again be whipped on, the horses are turning to stone.

THE WORKERS: AN ESSAI

Early on Monday, five AM, wintery darkness with December not even underway—*electricity*, because it's hard to get enough done, early enough, though those yearning to quit are in the minority—when the front doors burst open and the sidewalks teem with people rushing to the train station, the streetlamps (whip type) already seem to whimper as they suck the last dregs of energy from the wires; as though racked by fits of ague, they spit down bleared brightness on the hats of all the heads borne along beneath them; mindful of the rising per-capita light consumption in each of these premature winters, everyone knows that the power stations are already working at full throttle, the factory halls are about to open their doors wide; *energy*, the halls, already heated through the night, brightly lit and warm, are awaiting the workers' imminent arrival, the tool drawers strain to open, the hammer- and file- handles seem poised to leap into grasping hands; concentrated energy, amid streets still shaking to the drumming feet of all the hurried workers, amid work-bound cars' paths still intersecting dizzyingly, amid the still-unbroken processions of cyclists nearly shunted into the gutter. Arduously suppressing their morning smoker's coughs, with briefcases full of sandwiches, with breadbags dangling from their shoulders, with thermoses of coffee in their jacket pockets, the workers, columns of them—tides that barely part before the honking, trundling cars—cross the factory grounds, immediately filling the changing rooms, where the ruckus sets in, the clatter of the locker doors, the voices greeting stragglers with mockery so shrewd even at this early hour—*the workers' irrepressible sense of humor* (Friedrich Engels)—and one last time, at 5:25, a disconcerting smell spreads in the changing rooms: bed warmth that the bodies still seem to give off, arduously ignored by the workers who, at 5:30 sharp, amid the howling of sirens, flood back into the factory halls, whose doors crash shut, and it begins, what the word *arduous* at last describes truthfully: the unleashed work of all the workers.

1

That work whose perfectly calculated architecture of activity and rest is acoustically mirrored in a firmament of noise beneath the glass roof…so compelling, in the hours before the breakfast break, that the workers soon find a symbolic form for their multifarious actions' subjugation to a higher power, and head off signs of weariness, by striking up choruses to the rhythm of the hammer blows, so that the engineering teams in their glass observation posts, monitoring the interplay of operations with a visible edge to their gaze, at last relax their furrowed faces, perceiving that their compositions will merge to yield a symphony in which all instrumental phrases complete one another.

2

Are the workers really these flattened monsters of tonality. —

Before the siren sounds for the morning break, all the sounds merge into a ponderous chorus that plumbs the last, still-dark corners of the factory halls and summons the hiddenmost things into the daylight. At this hour, the stokers emerge from the boiler rooms; each with the handle of a wooden crate hooked in the crook of his arm, shuffling, their faces already blackened by coal dust—trickling drops of sweat have cleared just a few streaks from the temples down the cheeks—they head to the tool store with empty milk bottles lined up in their crates to be exchanged for full bottles. Leaning on the ledge outside the service window, patiently awaiting their allotment of milk, they gaze down the halls, interior opening onto interior, and the noise streams into their ear canals as though through layers of cotton wool. Those ears are not responsive to the symphony's harmonies. As an outsider, the first things to strike the stoker are the musical breakdowns that seem latent in the orchestra's performance, catastrophic breakdowns that, if they came to pass, would cause entire phrases to collapse; the sudden, over-harsh whine of a grinding machine's magnetic table swiveling at the end of its trajectory yanks his gaze in that direction; the shriek of a spiral drill, lapsing into an alarming crackle, nearly makes him run for cover lest the shattering tool should send shards in all directions; but the coolant emulsion boiling off in stale-smelling vapors seems to hide the origin of the barrage, there's not much the stoker can see amid the bewildering welter of men and machines, the work-related precautions and safeguards that strike him as superfluous, untenable, mutually exclusive, theses posted on the walls in the most unsuitable places. The crane's warning horn makes him dodge to the side, he watches as several coffee ladies, pushing an urn on a two-wheeled cart, are brushed aside like chaff before his eyes, and the persistent horn seems bent on chasing him away as well, but then, somewhere else entirely, he sees the gigantic bed of what will become a lathe being set down with a dull, grinding crunch; the workers guarding it yell commands not meant for the stoker, and the dissonant chime with which the retreating crane hook swings one last time against the hollow cast-iron form elicits their loud curses. Once the rust-colored monster is finally at rest and the workers are safe from the crane, once they're standing around it in silence, their left hands resting on its iron ribs, the stoker perceives the deadly fear that fills them in their speechlessness, in their lack of guidance before the work begins, the work that towers before them with incoherent, frantically manifold demands, that's required to make the hammer-textured green of a new machine blossom from the rugged bed; that work is still dormant, holed up unchosen and unrecognized in their left hands on whose palms the cold metal seeks to freeze the sweat of resistance; their faces are pale, their gazes turned grimly inward. The stoker beholds the workers in a minute-long state of burnout, impervious to the menacing edge returning to the eyes of the engineers, whose facial furrows, growing sterner, are visible again behind the glass of their observation posts; they've raised their heads. Meanwhile the workers' previous piece of work is boxed in a shell of pale-yellow planks in the dispatch area, where the thunder of the hammers, their stormy echo, is still heard; the workers' creation that they'd come to love and tenderly care for has become a commodity; somewhere in Morocco, Haiti, or Denmark the machine will perform some unknown, perhaps shameful task, poorly oiled, ruthlessly run into the ground, surrounded by implacable timekeepers with stopwatches, and in the end perhaps even spat on by an exasperated, badly trained, badly paid lathe operator.

The stoker could have been one of those workers, but the economy's mechanical consciousness would have crushed him; now and then he'd have intuited a mental lapse in the language of the economy, but without being able to identify it. If a visitor from Mars had asked him what the people here were doing, he'd have replied that these people, known as workers, were producing machines to manufacture machine parts for assembling machines to manufacture other machines, which in turn, under the workers' aegis, manufactured machine parts to construct machines for machine parts, finally ending up with machines for manufacturing the oil cans required to oil the machines. — Questioned as to his own position, following a protracted elucidation of his function he would have explained that stokers aren't described as workers; their services serve the work of the workers. The workers claim, clearly with good reason, that their work's existence generates the genuine economic utility, i.e. money, that makes the stokers' services necessary in the first place. — The stokers object that as contributors toward decent working conditions, which include the maintenance of a certain level of warmth as documentable by energy bills, they are the ones who actually enable the celebrated results of the work of the workers. — Then you're nothing but *contributors*, you admit it yourselves, retort the workers, feeling secure in their decent working conditions, and they cite a lesson from labor history that makes the stoker think anachronistic thoughts. If a strike were to transpire in the dead of winter, so the workers claim, the stokers would be exempted to keep the factory buildings in working order for the aftermath of the strike; otherwise the walkout would, as a rule, take place in summer, when temperatures are such that stokers are notable by their absence; and in that situation they'd be redundant, the first ones to get thrown out by the strikes' warring parties. — But that means, say the stokers, that in a labor struggle, at least in winter, we might be the ones to tip the scales. — No, the workers reply; we'd tolerate the ones who want to *contribute*, but on condition that they ensure, to the extent possible, the factories' continued operation, in the event, you see, that we should seize control of them.

3

The workers' implacable thoughts drive the stoker away, he takes his milk bottles back to his workplace; the fires in the boilers have sunk alarmingly low, but the siren has summoned the workers to their break, and for now he sits down at the dust-covered table. Sensing that he hasn't been able to conclude his thoughts yet. — — When the break is over and the workers return, they'll feel the warmth fading, nearly dissipated; the stoker can't guess whether they'll complain to the engineers or whether the engineers themselves are monitoring the temperature in the halls; ultimately the stoker can't believe that the workers would complain about him, ultimately they ought to feel closer to the stokers than to the engineers. Should the engineers happen to inspect the boiler room, they'd find the stoker working away, the second siren that ends the break having punctured the

lull in the boiler room and made him jump to his feet;
they'd behold the stoker sweating and irate, hurling coal
into the furnaces, his face displaying outrage, as though
he can't explain how the loss of heat occurred. Wordless
but grim-faced, the engineers depart, visibly incredulous,
declining to concede the innocence that shines upon the
stoker's sweat-covered brow, perhaps already devising
punishments should another such incident occur, and
upstairs they tell the workers: The stoker's firing the
boilers again, in just a few minutes the heat will come
through. — By then the stoker's back at his table, damp
brow propped on black fist; it's true, he hasn't been able
to conclude his thoughts yet, no doubt about that, it's as
though he sent the missing phrases into the flames along
with the coal, there's a void behind his brow, above him
is the grinding weight of things thought long ago, the
sense of the economy's towering edifice bearing down
upon him.

And, all alone in the basement of this tower, he can't
visualize the motion of the two classes above him inter-
acting…or should he say the motion of the workers and
engineers interlocking…is this motion a battle, or is it
mutual understanding. — The engineers are his enemies,
that seems indisputable, proven each time they poke their
heads into his boiler room…if it were a battle, then, that
moves those two classes, it would be manifest that only
a misunderstanding, an accident of language makes the
stoker appear not to belong to the workers. — If it's a
battle, as certain things suggest, then, however monstrous

the thought, the workers and the engineers must have a mutual understanding that this battle exists…but that it never really gets underway, for it's a battle between the engineers' speech and the workers' speechlessness. The battle lies in the reluctance with which the silence of the workers fills up with the engineers' language material; that is all there is to it. The work of the workers is a thing absolutely dominated, actually brought into existence by the language of the engineers; the abolishment of that language, the development of an autonomous language would simultaneously abolish the status of the workers. — — But the work of the stoker is mental work, harboring in all its steps the germ of an autonomous language… should the speechlessness of the workers seize control of the factory, he, the stoker, could not be dealt with other than in the language of the engineers; the lacunae in his thoughts would once more go unfilled.

Mental lapses persist in the stoker's appraisal, terrible lapses; perhaps the reason lies in the existence of the factory management. That practically anonymous group whose heads he can barely name. Whose physical appearance seems unimaginable, as none of them ever descends from the glass suites at the very top of the tower, and if so, then certainly not all the way to the squalid boiler rooms. There lies the lapse in the ruminations that he can't conclude…of course his fires have long since subsided again. The subterranean sun that supplies the tower with warmth has ceased to shine, the flow of steam has died in the upward-shooting pipes. Heads are raised on all the tower's levels, listening warily as the water drains from the radiators' ribs, windows are slammed shut when the iron starts to radiate cold, even the lighting seems to darken. The stoker sits motionless, his gaze aimed upward, as though he could see through the basement ceiling, through all the tower's floors and corridors; up there above him is where guilt sits enthroned, the guilt for his exhaustion, his mental lapses, his cursed fate as a non-worker, the guilt for the dying of the sun in his furnaces. It's only fair that the coldest place right now should be up there, amid the flicker of a frosty winter sky, the chief, upward-tapering office is one he can but dimly imagine, the walls of glass, double glazed, as though with water flowing through them, the barely discernable wire filigree of the electric security system in the glass. All the offices below are visibly chilly, hands are reaching for the phones to declare war on the stoker, and he waits in his musty basement with its sheen of frost and damp, back turned to the fire whose remains have fed his wrath, angrily he sits where he is, a dusting of ash on his half-closed lids; as the last light strikes his brow he watches his shadow collapsing on the wall. His shadow moves and multiplies as though he wished to rise up in polymorphous form, but the tower's weight holds him down on the chair, the thoughts in his head resemble the darkly glowing, caving coal, sparks fly up, ah, right beneath the tower of authority, in the basement is where the insurgents forge their plans, twisting and turning words that sound menacing and symbolic as political slogans. —

The workers are in full agreement with the engineers; it's cold; though the doors of the factory have long since closed, winter is seeping into their uniforms. — —

The engineers' secretary came down to the boiler room. The woman's appearance in the doorway—she was about forty-five, stoutly feminine, even the youngest workers described her as quite good-looking; though she'd pulled on a white cardigan, her arms were crossed and she seemed to be shivering—made the stoker start up in alarm; he had no idea how long she'd been standing there, observing his frozen crouch, the no doubt hideous mental movements in the mirror of his face; in his surprise he rose and approached her, brow furrowed in exaggerated attentiveness, unsure how to ask what she wanted—later his expression struck him as exaggerated, his movement toward her pointless, since she was already heading for his table—he knew the workers called the secretary by her first name, but he'd never tried to find out if the same right applied to him; on the other hand, it would have seemed outlandish to use formal language with a woman whom everyone in the factory addressed familiarly. He stopped a step away from her, and she was an inch or two taller; to ease the tension in his face he feigned a yawn while pressing the back of his hand to his open mouth, and she looked down at him with slightly protruding eyes, the fine creases of the lids daubed with a touch of mild green eyeshadow, an earnest look, but he felt it was marred by a glimmer of revulsion; revulsion, he felt, that might portend a sudden transformation into love; if the basement's crumbling ceiling had suddenly let a shower gush down on the stoker, instantly washing the stinking clothes from his body, the woman would suddenly have grasped the extraordinary ease with which water and fragrant soap washed the crusts of filth from his skin, that turnaround to love could have happened in the blink of an eye. — I brought you your money, *sir*, the woman said, brushing past him and marching to the table. As he knew, women never set foot in the boiler room; it wasn't just that the stokers were likely seen as cranky and menacing, it was more due to the huge, bulging scabs of plaster that seemed about to crash down any moment. The secretary, known as a spirited person who could defend herself if necessary, was the only woman who strictly disregarded the taboo, yet she showed up in the basement just twice a month, on payday. The stoker, still inhibited but reassured that she'd come for mundane reasons, followed her to the table; the woman waited, bravely ignoring the dust on the table until the stoker had taken the money and signed the pay envelope; grasping the envelope by one corner, but still catching some dust from the tabletop on the painted nail of her index finger, she said as she turned to go: What a day we're having up there again, do you have any idea… — Yes, I do, said the stoker, which was a complete falsehood, he didn't know, because she didn't necessarily mean the poor heating; with one simple question he could have kept the woman there with him for the time it took her to explain. She left, and as she climbed up the stairs and out of view, he asked himself, as always, whether she'd looked back at him before vanishing. — In any event, the secretary was one of the phenomena that united the workers with the engineers. The secretary knew what kind of a day they were having, in utter contrast to him, the stoker. In the disputes that broke out afresh each payday at the long tables set up expressly for the purpose beneath the glass windows of the hall manager's office, where the workers sat smashing their fists down in the spaces between the coffee cups and the crimson-faced engineers stood— never availing themselves of the chairs provided for the meeting—and tried to talk above the workers' complaints with a muffled edge to their voices, it was the secretary who assumed the role of arbiter between the workers' speechless raging and the engineers' argot. Several times, when those meetings led to arguments over the inadequate heat in the factory halls, and accusations were voiced against the stoker, it had been the secretary who defended him, albeit from an apparent misconception of the true situation; her case rested on what she regarded as the lack of decent working conditions in the boiler room, which silenced the accusers. Working conditions was one of the phrases that united the workers and the engineers, so the secretary met with no objections; these conditions were something for which the engineers were responsible, and simultaneously the status quo in which the workers operated, but since this factory's workers enjoyed good conditions, they were ones on which no agreement could be reached with the stokers. —

This, perhaps, was where the missing conclusion of his thoughts lay, the lapse in the sense of a gap: because the stokers' *working conditions* were known to be poor, probably even unacceptable, they were not referred to as workers.

Today, because the money came, I realize how money is a surrogate for language, a dull, worn coin for each gleaming word.

And my pockets are filled with money, despite my poor work under poor conditions; money compensates me for the conditions of work and silence.

In the stokers' silence about their working conditions, the workers sense a language far below the level of their speechlessness, the infinitely wretched, standpoint-free language of machines that have already been discharged from their love.

Money created the logic of these relationships, and there has been no *attempt* to break out from that language, to break out from the conditions of the language of that thinking, from the basement of that language, to blow the basement of that thinking sky-high. In that basement of exhausted symbols. In which those exhausted, pinned-down words writhed. In which those cliches, like revolting body segments, joined to form endless slithering pythons…but no, if only they were snakes, instead they're heaps of wretched, branded words, gigantic heaps of verbal stock that's bought and paid for, machine words, spare parts of words from which machine words, word machines are assembled…to produce yet

more words, old words that distort thinking, seemingly
new words that are stale metamorphoses of old words…
the attrition proceeds inexorably, and these are all the
words there are. — All the same, the secretary, that language's secretary, had pointed the way to a fresh start
over which the word dignity resounded; but no one had
followed her lead. — — Climbing the stairs, the stoker
poked his head out of the boiler room and saw that the
tired words of the meeting, kneaded to bits, had quashed
the arguments; it was quiet, and the victors, the engineers,
were back behind the glass of their offices. Amid the
scattered papers on the tables, pay envelopes, diagrams,
plans, the workers sat hunched over their cold coffee
dregs, their voices muted, reduced to an incomprehensi-
ble rasp, and scraps of symbols, briefly whirled up from
their desolate, disorderly heaps, sank wearily back into
place. The workers had plainly been told to go back to
work, and in a moment they would, clearly lacking any
choice in the matter…the stoker on the stairs, his head
just above the hall's cement floor, felt the cold, the real
cold that he himself had caused, the cold of the winter
that had seeped into the factory. That was the sole subject
that his language was supposed to address, the winter
that loomed in the red midday light outside the factory
doors, the winter that he had to cope with, because that
was his *work*. Silenced, he went downstairs to the basement: whether I'm just a contributor or, like any other
worker, a fighter of this factory, it makes no difference,
pondering the question has no point, it just whirls up

those old words again. The standpoint of the engineers, my superiors, is that I'm supposed to cope with the winter; that's the language that's been forced on me, and in keeping with that language I will return to the *operation of work*…like all the workers up there. With or without mental lapses: if the only option left is to operate from the standpoint of the engineers, that either means that *we, the workers*, are utterly without rights, without the right even to our own standpoint, one belonging to us, the workers; or, as seems sufficiently proven by the fate of our thinking, it means that the standpoint of the engineers, that is, the standpoint of the operation, is also our standpoint, the only standpoint possible for us, and that would mean that we, *the workers*, are nothing other than this *operation*…which we could understand, even accept, if only our brains were capable of converting this entirety, which appears as such a vivid fact before our eyes, into the standpoint of our, the workers', success, allowing us to stand as free men, upright at last, in the midst of all the work.

And to finish, an attempt to describe the end of the day, the way home. But the way home is no good for anything but the reuse of those old, worn thoughts. Anyway, it's the mirror image of the path taken in the morning, and that morning path—assuming you already inhabit the language of those final reflections—is the real way home. — The way back remains an irresolute path on which you're crushed by exhaustion, a treacherous path beneath the winter sun that you don't see, but in whose light you yearn to escape from everything, from the exhaustion of logic, from the operation, from your thoughts. From your clothing and at last, like Judas, from your own skin, against which your filled pockets burn.

THE READER

The reader, if he existed, would be this entity: a person, viewed from behind, hunched at a desk under a powerful lamp, mostly unmoving, with or without glasses, with or without eyes, head visible or invisible. With a ruled notebook on the desk in front of him, he fills line after line with a rapid hand, nimbly leafing through the pages until, finished at last, he rests his brow on the filled notebook; a deep sigh, saying that nothing can extinguish what has once been written. — Night fell long ago with all its blue weight, it's summer, a late summer in a late century, the window's ajar and moths have flown in, hurling themselves with audible clinks against the glass of the lightbulb. — All the while the reader hunches over the open book, who knows if he's reading, he's never turned a page, he might have fallen asleep, or he's the still-seated shadow of the man who rose from the chair; the black and white pages shimmer through his colors. If he were the reader, he'd sit broken at the desk with hands that have slipped from its surface, with frail drooping shoulders, hair falling over his glasses. Yet from every word in the host of hieroglyphs filling the pages, a voice would seem to whisper urgently to wake the reader. — Who, if not he, insofar as he existed, would wish for the end of the night to come; it's as though the lamp were losing power, darkness creeping in through its wires. — And the reader hunches over the book, his hand leafing, leafing through the pages. Calmly at first, waiting patiently a while between each pair of pages, then more impatient, leafing faster, faster, page after page he turns, with a pale face full of wrath and fear, with clenched fists frenziedly turning whole sheaves of pages, with his shoulders, with his lowered head, nearly wailing, he thrusts and shoves and forces aside the white pages mounting to walls, but not a word, not one letter does he find on the empty sheets. — If the reader existed, with just his eyes, no, with fire and sword, with just his mouth he'd spew all his words into the empty book. Inextinguishable, down to the sigh that crowns the work's completion at last with liberation.

HALF AN AUTUMN

Ians   for M.

Last night in the dark, one saw a birch's white trunk; abrupt from the grassland it...its white boughs slant-wise up, one saw the pale-gray fume of foliage, or it was a spray springing from the trunk, or the trunk sprayed and sprang, white were the branches, truly white was the bridge. *One* saw it clearly, yet I saw only half of everything.

Since it's impossible to hide behind an invented character, considering how far time has progressed, how long since we passed the zenith...since there's no ignoring the first person that begins every sentence, it's a gratuitous act of violence to explain why so many statements won't let us complete them, for that first person shapes them so exclusively that even so small a word as *loomed*, in sentence with an I, inevitably leads all the way to Babel...today's genius is indistinguishable from today's moron, therein lies the violence. Gnawed by night-gas, the throat speaks, see the lake one last time, see how it rises, how it loses its shores. See the whole of it, the view of the far shore was hubris...weary of an obedient future, sick of ceding the field beneath the brain-pan to a censor from the beyond.

A brook that flowed into the lake gathered pale mist-masses over its calm water, filtering like snow into the towering bales of the bushes, lamps mounted on tele-graph poles illuminated the ghostly chaos, and upon the flowing mists all at once there appeared, as on a second airy level of reality, more black gleaming leaves seeming to sprout from breath-clouded mirrors. After I'd passed a slicing wall of light, and, still blinded, crossed a stretch of shadows, I saw the lake, and above me the half-circle of a high white-painted bridge, an old backdrop, but to me the bridge seemed purely imaginary, only the upper part of its arch was visible, its feet, on either side of the brook, vanished in the blackness. A human construction, a framework of concrete and white-painted metal, only the top part intact in the lamplight, resting on both in-visible shores. An old internal method of mine compelled me to see everything only halfway.

The unmoving water, just beyond the phantom bridge it, before the brook merged into the, lake already shoreless, as I too, abruptly on a tiny patch of dirt and grass, marooned on an island sinking in the mists amid erratic currents, I found myself in shoreless, unmov-ing water just past the brook mouth, where it seemed to rise to great heights, into a darkness unknown all around, unnoticed in past nights without sleep and waking, a light, shoreless, shore-long; how in one single sentence the night described itself transformed into water; the rising moon, trembling at its edge, a disc distinct as neon.

I didn't dare press onward, as though afraid to go the whole way too soon, I knew that suddenly one's wandering unconscious in the unseen, planting one's feet in the heights between the stars, weightless, casting off one's precious weight; one rises, *lans*, head-down over the stars, overhead the deep water, underfoot the deep sky. I swayed, turned away, I grasped the railing of the bridge, damp scabby metal, a breath of air stirred, making the water gleam, the stars in it lengthened to fissures of light, some bird cry startled from sleep scraped my senses.

I'd scented the summer's fragility, the terminal humming in the metal of the vowels that I could feel stuck so detachably in my throat, that had a tang of aluminum... that indefinite but essential after-effect of sleeplessness from which I counted off muddled rhymes to myself, from which, lest I be forced to sell to myself as my own customer an utterly mercenary realism, I would either have to return to antiquated words, *ghostly*, *ghastly*, *grizzled* (though not long ago, reading old Russian books— implicit rededication to a long and happier epoch of my language—I'd noted an utter refusal to use such words to make sense of reality; but in the late fragility of my affiliations *literature* appeared as an alternative to language), or be damned to silence...I perceived the end of the season, not without the hoped-for artificial loftiness, when, pouring red wine one morning, I glimpsed in the very first glass a hair that had clearly emerged from the bottle, floating as though on a film of grease, distinctly recognizable, in thickness and curl, as a pubic hair; I poured the wine down the drain, instantly the sink was washed with bright red, sending up a stale-sour, metallic smell. That was the end, all my strength and fierceness vanished, I was no longer robust enough to endure the summer's faintly spoiled smell, the tiniest tainted drop sufficed to fatally infect me.

I'd been overzenithed by an artificial reality, and I had to get back to the bottom of things, had to part water from earth again, if need be rename the old light by which I did so.

Nevertheless I got drunk on the same wine that same day, couldn't sleep again that night and went out in the dark, cicadas and frogs, the rustle of leaves that had withered to paper, nothing but noise I'd already grown unused to, I sensed that I'd cast off nature, cast off my head-down consciousness…which at last, it seemed, was more unnatural even than nature.

Fooled by moon and neon, I walked swaying, once again that aluminum taste, aluminum smell in the mucous membranes, it was the same gray oxide that glittered on a metal fence, in the dim glow of the lights strung up there, at my back the black park, before my eyes the red, yellow, blue lights, between which I looked down into a large sports stadium, center of the late-summer park festival that was drawing to a close, its hubbub ebbing early that Sunday evening; down there, as well, lights linked the black leafy mountains of the treetops; the smell of paper lanterns burning somewhere in the grass, the slimy smell of sausage stands gone cold, the clink of glasses being washed in a zinc tub, a single burst of bleating laughter.

The bridge had let me cross the brook, not thirty years till the end of the century, and still no renunciation of that reality that never truly began, still no real beginning to that inevitable other half, so let's be off, let's cast off from it all, that was the point of the laughter that warmed me, and back to the town with its decrepit new buildings, neobuildings, windows mostly dark already, though in a few, as pitiable relics of the will to illusion, cheap fluorescent tubes between curtain and window are switched on to illuminate the house plants, the aquariums, a dim music-hall violet driving Impressionism to despair, and as the aluminum oxide flakes from the facades' sick skin, I sense the clinical gleam of the chemically treated tiles, the perfumed toilets, the nylon underpants soaking in the sink.

(Ghostly, ghastly, groundless. Shoreless sensation of my ancient disgrace. The lost proof. Bazarov, if only you could come and punch me in the nose. But you're rotting, done in by antediluvian frogs, you wasted *nihil* under your white birches.)

The mahogany-grained pressboard wall units, the trash bins plastered with Marlboro labels, the bookshelf with the *Abridged Encyclopedia of Health*.

Acceptance. I'm off, away from my youth's splendid season, away from seeing the whole thing, away from the crickets. What was really white was the bridge…in the daylight, I'd seen how the old crusts of its paint layers blistered, brown from the gnawing of the rust underneath, and many of the blisters had already burst, openly revealing the sickness; the red-brown scabby wounds spread, and only in the valleys between them did the white paint prevail, blackened by the entire summer's greasy dust; real paint, its blight doing justice to its reality…over the bridge I'd returned from a once-sacred wilderness, and the hope that the bridge would collapse behind me went unfulfilled. The town that lay before me, that I'd beheld in anticipation of the pestilences I'd partake of there… like a forgotten cloister garden I'd have to fill it, in a mystical act, with the chaos words of Genesis. For those cicadas under the resounding firmament could no longer be lulled to sleep, the night a hollow cavity, the hollow singing of summer, *lans*, a tuning, an open beginning. The dark sobbing of waters reduced to a puddle. In which too now, one believes, in the nights of undiminished heat, lakes are great reservoirs that influence the weather, how artificial, if one recalls the most natural things, in sentences, one believes, visibly riven by lightning-like malformations that portend the unseen half, the hollow shapes of the nights, rearing like cathedrals shading into blue, which the believing spirit enters amid astral electricity, Luna suddenly, filled the whole puddle, blinding white-kindled water where dead trees spun, torn loose.

Artificial primordiality, cicada weather, thought up by the moon brain, under the pallor of the mental

firmament where day breaks over rapid far-from-human
sentence fragments describing the collapse of the town,
under the neomoon, half
    seen and off again,
    the beginning is open

II

HE

Just then a chilly rain sprinkled from the sky as low-hanging clouds gathered again, and it occurred to him, leaving behind the last houses in the upper part of town and already catching sight of his goal, the nearby village in the broad valley below, that it looked like stormy weather, and it would be wiser to postpone his visit to the village until some other day. At that very moment, as he was about to slow his steps, a woman's voice called from a house off behind him, blurting out the words in rapid succession: Don't take this road any farther, my good man, go back, you'll be doing yourself and all of us a favor. — That's just what I was about to do, he replied with a smile, the way one parries a rather disarming joke. But as he turned, heading back toward town, he saw that all the houses' windows and doors were closed, except for one dim vestibule whose door stood ajar, but there, too, not a soul was to be seen. Perhaps the woman's voice had been a mere trick of the senses; then it was embarrassing that he'd replied out loud. But no one seems to have heard me, he told himself, and groping for the vest pocket of his coat he thought, what a good thing that I put my papers in my pocket when I left the house, the woman's words were so sharp and arbitrary, she might just as well have ordered me to identify myself. When he looked up at the clouds, they were drifting low and dark along the downward-sloping road, over the lower part of town; several birds flying that way scudded along so arrow-swift that it looked like black wires stretched through the air beneath the sky. Though he felt he should quicken his pace, he took the time to glance over the front hedges at the exhausted stems of already-unpetalled tulips and dense lilac bushes whose purple blossoms were turning brown; in the window of one of those mansion-like houses from the time before the war, a curtain seemed to move, and he walked on, not wanting to disconcert the inhabitants by peering into their gardens. Encountering a gaggle of children at play who'd chalked large squares onto the sidewalk, he moved toward the curb so as not to step on the squares, but the children stepped in front of him. Pausing in their game, they watched him in silence, with what struck him as astonishment, and the oldest, best-dressed boy said with an utterly unchildlike severity: You'll have to use the left side of the road, sir, you're prohibited from walking here. — Nonplussed, though more by his hand's involuntary fumble for his papers than by the child's open insolence, he swallowed the retort on the tip of his tongue, noticing a barely perceptible movement in the curtain behind one of the windows; no doubt the boy reckoned on solid support from the houses' adult inhabitants; there was nothing childish in his even, unfaltering gaze, but rather total faith in his right to make that monstrous demand. Now that the first raindrops could be felt, it was better not to linger unnecessarily, and with a rather awkward smile he headed for the left side of the road, but there the sidewalk ran atop a high embankment, climbable only by stairs a long way apart, so that he had to walk a good hundred yards in the gutter of the muddy road, and when he looked up at the houses on that side, he seemed to sense laughing faces behind the curtains. To make matters worse, an automobile came racing up the road so recklessly that his trousers and shoes were instantly spattered all over with mud. At the top of the hill the car turned sharply and returned at an even faster clip, this time in the wrong lane, spattering him to the hips again, passing so close that the wind made him stumble and catch himself in the embankment's muddy grass to keep from falling down. And so an old fool nearly meets his death on an innocent walk, just because he stupidly used the filthy road instead of the clean sidewalk, he thought in a fury, and quickened his pace at last, driven onward by the wretched sight of his spoiled clothes, by the intensifying rain, by the people's mocking laughter that he fancied he heard, and by a soft singing that buzzed in his ears, the hum of fine imaginary wires in the air, touched off by wind and rain, spreading the news of his plight across town. Promptly, and with still swifter strides, he turned onto the next side road, more a broad sandy

path, though it would take him still farther from his
home, which he meant to reach the long way around just
to avoid that ill-fated road. But on the side road stood
the car that had just barreled past, a broad-beamed black
sedan; a door opened and a tall, youngish man hurried
out; coatless, wearing a pale gray suit of a delicately
shimmering plaid over a pale pink shirt, adorned with a
dark red, fluttering tie, he seemed clothed with a
deliberate understatement that underscored his urgent
haste; but then again with an overcalculated effect as,
leaving the door open, shouting inaudible instructions
back at the chauffeur, he approached and, barely checking
his stride and immediately heading back again, neither
heeding the other man's confusion nor seeming to expect
a reply, called: You'll have to turn back, young man, as
fast as you can, you must have seen that this road is going
to be blocked. — On this road there was no sign of a
roadblock. Besides, *young man* was inappropriate; the pale
gray gentleman was obviously much younger than him.
— Well, get on with it, turn back, the younger man
repeated, this time in a sharp, menacing tone, while yet
another, older-seeming gentleman got out of the car and
strode forward just as resolutely, only to stop again and
wait for the first man, whereupon the two of them,
glancing at each other and then shaking their heads as
though at some signal, got back into the car, which drove
away at once. — Now it's too late, he thought, stopping
indignantly; I really am what everyone here takes me for,
a fool that any child can blindside. Why didn't I demand

an explanation. I could have demanded an apology, yes, I could even have lodged a complaint somewhere else—but apparently it's already too late to think of that—no, I could have demanded that they show me their IDs. — But he had no idea where that *somewhere else* might be, the place to lodge his complaint, he sensed that the same people who'd blindsided him would be waiting for him there. — He felt he'd been standing here for longer than he could think, suddenly he found it revolting to make someone *show their ID*, what a revolting invasion, he thought, isn't it bad enough to have to carry those brutal documents around with you. — These are thoughts like the movements of marionettes, he mused, and it's scandalous, really, that we've come to resort, at the least provocation, to this system of revolting methods. — He was back on the road he'd just left, and after just a few steps back the way he'd come, he found himself faced with an actual roadblock. A ditch had been dug across the entire road, with several men at work in rubber raincoats, a ditch so deep that only their heads showed, and they seemed too busy to notice him. Later he couldn't remember if he'd spoken to the workers, maybe asked them to lay a plank over the ditch to let him continue on his way, or whether his voice had caught in his throat. At any rate, the workers didn't even seem to see him, and already it was too late. With screeching brakes the black sedan stopped behind him, and the young man in pale gray jumped out. — That's enough now, he heard the stern voice, get in the car. — At once he saw that resistance was pointless and, trembling, awkwardly hampered by his coat, he took a seat in the back, unable to ignore the young man's disapproving look at the dirt that his shoes left on the car's floor mat. In the back seat he had to squeeze between the two men's bodies, and the car leaped forward even before the door closed, hurling him against the seat back, where he felt two shoulders pinning him. Where are you taking me, he finally ventured to ask, but received no reply. Instead, the young man in pale gray leaned over him, shimmering soft jacket pressing against the dark of his coat; as that face suddenly loomed close he felt its gaze meet his, but the eyes were quickly averted when he searched them for an answer, or merely mercy, in front of his face the gray man's slender hand executed a vague, apologetic wave before slipping lightning-quick under his lapel; in alarm he sensed the warm deft hand, felt it unerringly seize and pull out his identity papers. Without a look inside, the gray-plaid man hid them in his jacket and, leaning back in his seat, lit a long, obviously expensive cigar, sighing in relief as though an unpleasant duty had been dispatched. — Where we're taking you, the reply came at last, when his question already seemed nearly forgotten, and the one deigning to respond was the older of the two men, whose job it must have been to do the talking now, is where the right path is, we'll show you soon enough. — The marked irony, the bad grammar, the rude tyrannical words, all of it made him shudder; now, he realized, every protest, indeed every question would be used against him.

Meanwhile, the car raced along at a furious pace, the rain came down so hard that nothing could be seen left or right beyond the streaming panes; next to the driver's head, through the arc cleared by the windshield wipers, he saw the dark leaves of trees or bushes shoot past, now and then a house; this went on for a long while, the car's tires singing on the asphalt like wires. Once, when the car stopped, motor running as though about to leap forward, there was a din as of great iron gates opening, and then the journey went on, helplessly, swiftly, and maybe for a long, long time.

ST. JOHN'S EVE

I'm soliloquizing with the light, a luminous breath of air in my brain dispelling dread and fatigue.

Lingering light between the window bars, brown dusk in the cell, brown fumes envelop me on my bunk, overwarm sweat-fuming blankets heavy with death-brown damp from which the death-sodden silence rises, brown as the tobacco of the dead, ethereal, proven as silence only by the soft cautious snores of the frail sleeper beneath me—a twenty-two-year-old, semi-illiterate pedo with a mental age of twelve—who irregularly, laboriously presses shallow breaths from his ravaged lungs, brown breath filled with saliva drops, a wheezing that by morning will have formed a dry, salt-like rim around the fissured corners of his mouth.

The same thing happens every night; in a while my other cellmate will wake up, listen a moment to the sound of the snoring, and then, in a fit of temper, believing it was the soft snores that woke him, lower his hand to the floor to grope for a shoe and slam its heel over and over against the iron frame of our bunk bed, at which the

73

snores, already tentative, will instantly fall silent; without waking, the sleeper beneath me holds his breath a long time, for nearly a minute there's no sound in the cell; apart from the angry tossing of the roused second cellmate, paralysis and quiet prevail, fear possesses the boy beneath me, it fills his sleep utterly, the heart seems to falter in that puny body. My other cellmate is about thirty, with several previous assault convictions, a burly, coarse-boned figure on oddly spindly bow legs, his long arms, tattooed to the shoulders, always dangling limber and pugnacious; he's the hero of hair-raising fist-fight scenarios, his victories in these brawls constitute his sole, inexhaustible topic of conversation, with wild gesticulations and imitations of his opponents' cries of pain accompanying his stories, and the little guy below me listens all day long in anxious admiration.

Before my other cellmate dozes off again, loudly gnashing his teeth in his sleep, a ferocious noise that drowns out the little guy's soon-resumed snores, a noise will emanate from the direction of his bunk—his is the only bunk in our cell equipped with a spring frame—a soft rhythmic creak lasting barely a minute, caused by the nightly round of masturbation knocked off between his first and second sleeps, ending in a painfully suppressed gasp that merges seamlessly into the tooth-grinding of his second sleep.

Later, surely, I'll encounter astounding numbers of people on the street whom, though strangers, I'll seem to recognize, with instantaneous, nearly mortal alarm, as the spitting image of one of my two cellmates.

The thin, rachitic body of a far too young, nearly flat-chested mother will display the erratic movements of the pedo; like his, her actions will miscarry from sheer doubt as to the point of them, and nearly always be aborted prematurely, so that glasses, spoons, or playing cards will fall to the ground, grasped too hesitantly or merely brushed; and later I'll discover in the protruding eyes of a person unfamiliar to me—but rendered familiar by the congruity with my sojourn here, which by then shall lie in the past—a sexual predilection for immature things, botched techniques, devices rendered nearly unusable by their incomplete construction, and though these things will give him grief, he'll buy them all the same. — Here they give us unbreakable plastic cups to use. — Or, possibly in more people still, in countless people who'll later cross my path, I'll find the semblance of my other cellmate, the thug, in the chin, severely shaven and covered with tiny cuts, of a still-young man in a green, tailor-made, jeans-style suit with patch pockets set off by white stitching, greased hair severely parted above his face, cut noticeably askew behind his bare ears; I see him in the supermarket, his powerful hands delicate for a moment as they pick and choose among different tubes of shaving cream… no, that's not how I'll recognize him, it'll be by analogy to the way he walks ahead of me slightly stooped, tilting his head back, during our free time in the prison yard each morning, completing his thirty-three circuits of the volleyball court with arms hanging motionless, slightly bent at the elbows, fists permanently clenched; later I won't have the faintest notion how that human stride in front of me could have been an inexhaustible daily cause of inarticulate inward screams of horror lasting minutes and mounting to piercing shrillness, how I had to turn away and gaze at the barred, arched windows of the hulking gray building as though at some place I keenly yearned to return to; for that stride in front of me, in those ever-polished shoes, is marked by an indescribably assured, infallible automatism—which in a later Now lacks all description but *senseless horror*—with steps not an inch too short or too long, an image that keeps tripping me up on concrete free of the slightest obstruction, keeps threatening to make my face collide with the unperturbed backs in front of me; whereas I start to limp after just four or five circuits, my two cellmates walk shoulder to shoulder like a single figure, the separation of their persons discernable only when the big guy hisses an unintelligible word into the other's ear, at which the little guy, smiling in approbation, turns his head to the inside of that double figure; otherwise their heads look forward mutely, and I know that they're filled with the most ingenious plans: every Thursday after showering they'll snag the most expensive, most strongly perfumed cosmetic articles from the meager selection the staff have on offer. — Once I was seized by the conviction that I'd be bound to recognize the bigger of my cellmates buying a television in an electronics store. Paralyzed by horror, I'd inescapably recognize a stranger's coarse hand, scornfully bent back in pride, with the distinctive split nail of the thumb on the sales slip hiding the index finger; electrified by panic in the wake of that horror I'd bolt out of the store, pressing myself in senseless fear into the niche of the shop window, and the TV sets displayed in that window would stare at me with pupils white-gray from cataracts, but seeing me all the same, mirroring my shrunken image in infinite sequence, all the programs of their sensory innards indelibly recording me, cheek pressed to the wall, plotting to murder the man who'd step out the door a few moments later.

Just before the voice of the outside light at the window fades, the human voices inside the prison's body seep away as well, though for a long while the walls, like sponges, let every sound flow through their pores…in the lengthening evenings all the channels of a *pretrial detention center* are filled by *sentences with no ends* that one's compelled to spin out endlessly…the vast, desecrated body of a monastery seems to have silently closed its doors to shut in every sound of the Black Masses and infernal processions unfolding inside that walled organism; all the fragmentary stirrings that a moment previously had disclosed the most inward, secret things, before all the listening windows, to one single waiting ear in some unknown cranny of the organism; all of it subsides into a silence in which, from now on, ideological devilries brood in each fate-cell, severed even from the adjacent fate-cell that by day had dwelled in vague familiarity. On the surface the silence is suddenly transformed into the outside, the noise of the town, so close, but insurmountably walled off from *us*, the taunting honks of the cars, the dexterous silencing of their transmissions followed at once by the ruthless revving of engines at the intersection that's close but invisible from the window; the distant but rapidly approaching sirens of ambulances or police cars: too laaate, too laaate; *laughter*, it takes a long time for sleep in the cells to overcome the outside.

Before this silence falls—as its prologue, lending it meanings that, though inexplicable, instantly begin their long work in all the minds: loud fragments along the building façade, the information exchange *necessary* for the organism's individual cells: one two here Cocker got you by the short hairs…in a pig's eye…how much… three tobaccos…fine how much…petition Hans two Steve one six buddy one four aaappeeeal…shut your face…dig in…

At intervals, laughter…I've never heard laughter as often as in this organism…at intervals, it must be a very distant cell, a braying unmelodic chant consisting of one endlessly repeated line: I ain't gonna work on Maggie's farm no more…the voice tries to bray the word *farm* like Bob Dylan, truncated and slurred, and it sounds like some unfamiliar word called faamn…faamn…

Amid the organism of this world, of this time, a language fit for human beings can consist only of unended sentences.

Freedom to find your own end is something that even the most felicitous system cannot guarantee, and beginning early in the morning you're forced to resist the linguistic processes that seek to dispose of you...an aaapeeeal for the words.

When my interrogations came to an end, and the affidavits incriminated neither myself nor any acquaintance not yet arrested, I knew that sooner or later I would be set free.

With my two cellmates, who knew nothing of these conclusions in my mind, I sat on a stool at the folding table that morning, after breakfasting on the leftovers of the previous day's cold supper, supplemented at a certain hour by a round of coffee; we smoked our arduously procured, lethal tobacco from the only pipe we owned, waiting for the words *free time*, which, at a moment we could not anticipate—no one in prison ever learns the time of day—would come indistinctly through the peephole to dictate the imminent twenty- or thirty-minute march around the grassy volleyball court...but nothing happened except the measureless light of summer lancing through the cell from the barred windows, the summer reaching its zenith outside the building; the acacias, crazy unpruned street trees that some distance away thrust their sprawling loads over the yard's barbed-wire-topped walls, had turned a visibly darker green with the slowly waning days; we sat and said nothing, and nothing happened—sitting on the fourth stool or lying on the free fourth bunk was death, whose perpetual presence we'd barred from speaking, who didn't dare challenge us to a gambling match—we were ready to jump up, to embrace each other with cries and tears, but were prevented by the conclusions in my head, which would end the sentences we spoke here; meanwhile the light was so strong that it blanched the rising plumes of tobacco smoke, and our bodies dried out, our smell of shit and urine, food and pomade burned off; paper and a pencil lay on the table, but we wrote nothing and said nothing, knowing that a single, random sentence would turn us into raging beasts, we'd lunge to tear each other apart tooth and nail; the proof of all words was lost...I sought a simile in the light's unnameability, I sought to compare it with the light of the evenings that often took so long to melt against the window bars, but now it remained nameless and measureless, a light that seemed to illuminate our corpses, to sever our brains from us, and it remained answerless until it turned toward the blood-hued fire of sunset; the beginning of my thoughts was the middle of the year, the time of midsummer, St. John's Eve, with divinely short nights that were full of promise and preserved the sun in the center of a liquid twilight, the beginning...the long-drawn-out sound of a rare, remote madness encompassing the thoughts that have fled...in which the hills glow in magical fires and the tombs are opened when the lower world utters its sentence, interrupted by shards of blood-soaked shrouds, whose earliest words I, cut off, but I, have heard, be free, I repeat, be free you who are dead, I greet you, I greet you

all, you earth-sodden bodies, I'm going, faamn, catch fire
at last, don't work, don't ever work no more in the yards
and the gardens of authority, I must turn away and walk
until I'm recognized in the streets of the angry towns,
mistaken for another, stricken down, as the stranger who
has long dwelled within me, recognized by an innocent
gesture and murdered, for the sake of the fatal recognition
brought by a forgotten sentence that cheated you of the
last of your tobacco, I will go, for the gates of that stone
body will open up before me, so that I may step out to
face the end, the end of sentences, so that an authority
shall cheat me of the next sentence, of the perpetuation
of an endless choir, I greet you all, don't forget to collect
your watches on the way out...

THE PRECINCT OF PEACE

The day seemed reluctant to brighten, the morning gloaming lingered, a stony gray conglomerate of façades and low fog burdened me with breathless weight; my awakening remained doubtful even as that city loomed upon my chest. Despite the grotesque foreshortening of my legs and lower body, I could barely see my frigid feet, had to strain my aching neck to lift my gaze from the horizontal, and in that moment there was revealed to me the vision of an alarmingly close, yellow-brown massif that I instantly seemed to identify as egg-shaped, it was a mountain shaped like a colossal egg, like an egg's pointed half, rearing up into the clouds, there was no way to take in the whole of the monstrosity that I could only hope was dead; it was like a film of the near side of a planet that had come too close to the earth and was now retreating with infinite slowness; however high I aimed my gaze, like a camera, it failed to reach the top, and however far I lowered it, until my neck muscles cramped painfully, the underside, the bottom, the base of the object was not to be seen. Its curve could only be guessed at; whatever distance the object gained, there was no way to encompass the oval shape of its bulk, which seemed hostile to humanity. All the same, if I allowed my bewildered eyes to linger for a second, its front seemed to vibrate with mysterious life. Yet life was hardly the word for the movement detectable on that vertiginous precipice. Some of those stirrings faded so quickly that I perceived them, as it were, only in hindsight, conceiving them as the ineffable, fickle existence of light reflexes, unexpected gleams like roaming sunbeams flung back by glass panes, and sometimes the barely perceptible glimmer of wispy blue-white smoke dissolving in a moment of sun.

The lofty wall that loomed before my face—seeming all the loftier since I was lying on my back with my feet stretched out toward it—was covered with semioval huts, tiny in proportion, that I recognized as dwellings only by the black entryways; the entire wall seemed to consist of huts, fused together, nested under and over each other, the base of one always resting on two or three huts that adhered beneath it, and so on, with no apparent paths or stairs in between; the entire wall was a hive composed of these abodes, superficially resembling a gargantuan leprous eruption—fissured, discolored, but unquestionably sculpted—through which the substrate, the rock of the mountain peak that had to be holding the whole thing together, was nowhere visible. Had there not been signs of fire and smoke, presumably also metal and glass, had it not been for the rational, thoroughly geometrical imbrication and interlocking whereby each hut kept the others from plunging to immeasurable depths—so that ultimately everything was buttressed and upheld by its own power—I would have taken the whole thing for a prodigious bird colony, even more so because everything had an indefinite, vegetative hue and the huts resembled inverted nests built from the dung of herbivores.

There may have been no real proof, but I was gazing at the abodes of intelligent beings, a people utterly free of vertigo that had defied gravity to find its natural habitat on the sheer face—only gradually inclining toward an oval's curve—of a mountain that reached the heavens. The Asiatic aspect of those myriad huts, the corresponding vastness of that settlement whose bounds I could not descry, the Tibetan quality of those heights—whose atmosphere was finally suffused by the mild red light of a sun rising in invisible reaches—seemed manifest to me; I believed it imperative, bizarre yet natural, to connect the vision to the Himalayas, for that artificial scab, now yellow-brown, actually the color of excrement, at last truly teeming with life, posed an enigma whose existence seemed utterly natural, just as it still seems natural for the Asiatic and the enigmatic to be linked.

Now that I had seen the enigma clearly, yet actually failed to make out a thing, it sank into the barely perceptible haze, the high mountain haze of sun-flooded clouds, so its image threatened to slip from my grasp, to blur in the distance, even before I craned my neck to cast my eyes downward and finally saw the water. Beneath me, on a plane far remote from mine, I saw the mirror-smooth lake that surrounded the mountain's foot in an arc, so divorced, so detached from the civilization of huts that began with the mountain's rise from the water, that that civilization, like something utterly unreal, immediately assailed me by lapsing into oblivion. A sheer mirage, soon the pale blue waters would close over it once more in unbroken splendor, and over the surface, bent away from the already fading shore, a few slender, crescent-shaped sails would recede, their movement barely perceptible.

I wept, in a sudden clouding of my consciousness—as a second, cherished person dissolved out of me, or else a second, unlooked-for person entered my body to suddenly complete me—on the morning after my hard-won but ultimately unexpected release from prison, while listening to a Hebrew chant transmitted amid crackling interference by the old radio set in the filthy kitchen, grasping at last that it was my own self who'd been sent back to be present in a peace that left me cold. The psychological preparations for my release, which for more than two weeks had occupied me almost constantly, might have done me some good if they'd lasted a shorter time—

but the security officials who'd hinted at my release in vague, open-ended statements had either misplanned, or lacked the authority for such statements, which evinced a nearly unlimited power and the capacity to follow up with a reality barely hoped-for and hence all the more astonishing (I had to reckon with the statements' ambiguity; my potential discharge was announced on the proviso that I make my peace with the *authorities*, a peace stipulated as essential for my release; at the same time, however, I had to heed the subtext of the statements, which denied my release because my peace with the relevant authorities was a necessary condition inside the institution, namely for as long as it would take them to get an adequate grasp of the *case*, unimpeded by any attempts on my, the arrestee's, part to dictate terms by agreeing to cooperate in the clarification of my case only on condition of that release whose prospect they held out…that seemed more imperative than making my peace with the authorities outside the institution… furthermore, I had to assume that the security officials divined my awareness of the subtext, indeed, that they presupposed it…so as to keep their calculations in step with the arrestee's deductions, to continue to presuppose his conclusions and so on…when in fact his sole conclusion should have been reached long ago: *it's clear that I can no longer be justifiably detained*, but that's a conclusion of which the prisoner is soon incapable, in just a short time imprisonment forever relativizes one's trust in power, imprisonment is irrefutable proof that power places not the slightest value on trust), or the security officials' hints had some other purpose unknown to me, some new and unexpected tactic intended to mislead me (when the release did come, it was a Pyrrhic victory; now startling, like an ambush, it proved to the arrestee, once

again and utterly, the total, well-nigh despotic—for now
despotism alone was manifest—dominion of grammar
over his brain, which had failed him in the effort to cal-
culate the implications of a mysterious verdict…and he'd
have to go in peace, which would not have been possible
had he been released into a true freedom)

—but those fourteen days were too long, and so my
preparations self-destructed, all the calculations I'd based
on the grammar of meanings self-destructed, the peace
I'd resolved upon, when my sole aim was that release,
turned into its opposite, into a war against all inward
and outward causalities; now, following my release, I saw
that that grammar's purpose had been fulfilled, I grasped
the inevitability with which that purpose had occupied
my mind, despite all the calculations and counter-cal-
culations I'd employed to hunt it down and destroy it…
oh, I'd hunted it to the point where my power to think
abandoned me, where I grew weary, where the beginning
of my reflections, the point of my exertions had long
since slipped from view…it wasn't yet the end of the
possibility of thought, but the end of my circumscribed
ability to trace connections; in the middle of a gram-
matical crossroads I'd move on in one direction, hastily,
but merely reaching a new crossroads, from which I'd
keep on reaching crossroads, and so on, and all the while
tormented by the suspicion that I'd taken the wrong turn
at the very start of this galaxy…I'd walked those paths
sitting on the stool in my cell, had walked them in no
one's company but my own, and because I couldn't really

verify the paths' value, the stretches I'd covered crumbled behind me, dissolving, swimming in an ever-redder fog of rage; I began to see my own figure, but as though divested of mind, on many paths at once, all leading astray...I came to believe that the destruction of that grammar's apparent purpose—whose power grew in my skull like a painful, consciousness-altering tumor—was identical to the destruction of my will to peace, ergo, I could be released, criminalized at last by the destroyed peace that could now fill the void of my body; my release, my *going free*, would inevitably make me guilty, so that my release would be unjustified, and this would happen in some moment of my awareness of myself; my release would be reversable with my own consent, consent to the law whose text could now be used against me...and hence consent to my stay in prison; the war drummed into me, the war against myself would be won, won by my foe even before I'd called him my *foe*, and without his having aimed a single blow against me...and once I was released, I was surrounded by the fractious peace of the persons into whom I had split.

The weather over the roofs was a cold, damp peace; it was a frosty gray July, said to be the coldest in half a century; my tiled stove, long unused, clogged with ash, soot, and crumpled paper, its top rubbed to a shine with margarine wrappers, failed to warm the kitchen; smoke, together with the grease fizzling on the stovetop, filled the room with rancid blue fumes; I went out and climbed the stairs to the next floor to look out over the roofs of the back buildings and see if the countryside really had turned green. Far off, light fell from a low sky, enough to lend a yellow sheen to the gathering cloud banks; amid the shattered landscape of the ravaged strip-mines, the black-gray of slender, tattered strips of woods, threatened by the foam of the trash heaps from which, as from the surf of filthy seas, white tatters wafted into the trees, and stretching past the spits of land jutting into the strip mines, atop which ancient mine buildings or defunct briquette factories, brick red and caked with grime, seemed to defy the decay of their roofs—akin to the ruins of heathen citadels whose architecture, no longer intelligible, casts doubt on the utility of past intentions that have lapsed into oblivion—amid this vast wasteland, washed with a yellow-green anti-vegetation, wound the curves, paradoxically defined by no longer extant obstacles, of a passenger railway that I knew had gone bankrupt long ago and along which a freight train now crept, its locomotive spewing white clouds that were immediately forced down by the atmosphere and boiled away in the flayed landscape's hollows.

On that otherworldly plane above dark, staggered cloud layers closing over the earth's delineated face: the braziers beginning to burn.

If I were to shut myself up in my cold apartment again, I'd have to ignore the relentless anticipation of those papers lying on the table; I could do that only by fleeing into the expanses of a different time or accepting the fragmentation of my *I*, by being the one to whom those papers did not pertain—I'd gained experience in that while in prison—rather than the person on whom society's law had been imposed, a mindless law that, untethered from reality yet aping a law of nature, dictated the inseparability of body and mind and was bent on reintegrating the fraudulent wholeness of my *I* into the cold peace of the world, the cold peace that, like a low, horizontal sky, had gone gray over the freedom that was possible here, the freedom to shut myself away…I'd been summoned to take these papers and go with them to the district capital to reregister with the authorities, not knowing whether I'd be allowed to return unhindered, with the official stamps confirming my registration, or whether some more subtle restriction to my freedom of residence was in store or some new accusation drawn from an inexhaustible pool of possibilities would immediately result in my rearrest…if, then, in the apartment whose suddenly palpable size offered means of escape, in the scant hour left before the train departed, I could fraudulently disregard these papers, looking asquint, covering my eyes with the splayed fingers of one hand…a breath of light in my brain would suffice, and already these were no longer the fingers that belonged to me, and soon these were no longer the walls, the roof, there was a great singing of flames sensed above the cloud-roofs, a real singing banished from the earth, and once again Atlantis, the idea effervescing up from degradation… and it's possible for me to transform back, in one imponderable second in the twilight beneath my fingers, in the shadow of the bars, the landscape of memory spreads out before me. In the early noons in which that rain-light died, while starting to shine in the distant unknown, and leaving warm mists of brightness like water flowing down from newborn hills, there was the green clemency of new oxygen suspended over the crossroads. As my male body's secrets opened wide, and I suddenly seemed able to see in all life's different directions, either back to earlier woods sealed by the mist of the rain that had passed, or, as I desired, to the Mediterranean light of the solstice… and I was forced to choose between perfect ignorance and the overwhelming surfeit of knowledge inherent to a world that is ending…I felt something step up behind me, and I knew that a free act was near, an act for which I could not be punished, and that it was youth.

Struggling to raise my eyelids to form a crack of light for my pupils, I waged a hopeless battle with gravity; only if I conquered it would I become a different person; the pressure at my nape that locked my chin to my chest mercilessly shackled my senses, gravity was a sickness that had dwelled within me as long as I could remember, but that I forgot for long stretches until, in some unexpected moment, something reminded me, and the ensuing plunge into a bottomless abyss could be halted only by radically abolishing the *I* that I was in that instant.

Strangely, I was still standing at the window at the top of the stairwell, merely seeming to look out; as though to deceive myself, I persisted in the same stooped posture—but now with a foot propped on the windowsill—in which I'd held my ear to my front door to listen before stepping out into the stairwell. That was it, I was still listening for sounds in the halls of the building, silent in the morning hours, by no means did I want to encounter another person. With alarm I'd heard the street door open, it was the postwoman, busying herself with the mailboxes; I tried to recall which tinny or wooden rattle would signal that something had been dropped into mine, but I couldn't say; with relief I heard the postwoman leave the building without climbing the stairs.

Perhaps I'd been standing here for far too long, and people had already walked past behind me. Though I was trying to avoid any kind of encounter, it was they who slipped down the stairs behind me without a greeting, who didn't dare address me, as though I were the building's terrible new despot. Now came the revenge for the prurient curiosity with which they'd watched—poorly concealed behind the curtains, perfectly visible to me— failing to block the officers' path even for a second to ask about my plight (much less to say the slightest thing in solidarity), as, with the cuffs around my wrists, I was led to the van across a sidewalk that, in that moment, completely *derealized*. Their scrutiny from behind the curtains conveyed that there had to be some legitimate reason why I was being taken away so openly.

The derealized sidewalk…the ghastliness of that moment, which I sought so long to put a name to, precisely matched what I felt when the gravity of all things momentarily dissolved…I knew that yesterday, when I'd crossed the same sidewalk on my way back, everything ought to have repeated itself, perhaps unintelligibly, in reverse, thus enabling me to return for real. The fact that this hadn't occurred meant that the imprisonment that began at the moment of my arrest, when all urban geometries seemed to collapse in upon me and engulf me…I suddenly *beheld* a strange figure, delivered up to the chaos of rubble uprooted from all contexts, and that figure was myself, I beheld myself as though a possible subsequent memory of that moment had become one with the actual occurrence…that the culpability and disfranchisement of my person, transparently exemplified in the sudden dissolution of all that was solid, could not yet have come to an end…that I hadn't managed to transform back into a reputable person.

From the stairwell window he saw the six-foot-tall, all-too-familiar wall crowned with cemented shards of glass enclosing the rectangular, black, cinder-covered yard behind the anachronistic, Bauhaus-style barrack-like structure that housed the elementary school. That yard was referred to as the school garden (for cultivating children's budding bodies, he concluded, and he knew of no one who'd left that yard eight years later other than as a slave), and he saw himself, overseen and directed by loathed or unrequitedly loved female Young Pioneer leaders, amid the marching formations, three abreast, as they made their slow circuits of the cinder yard between lessons. In front of this wall, at the edge of an unpaved, perpetually muddy street, the nightshade tree was still standing, growing with undiminished vigor though its trunk had been split by shrapnel in the war, and it was now in late bloom, glowing gray-pink. The wall had gone unscathed by the war...you're still the one who's made to stand with his face to the wall, the wall of the schoolyard, the wall of the building, remember that, your face turned to the red-brown fired glaze of the neatly grouted bricks that the war left unscathed...inmate, you know you've got to stand with your face to the wall, what goes on in this building is none of your concern... remember that that injunction means you won't be in this building forever. — The school's large, rectangular structure had presented an obvious target in the air raids, but it had been spared, in stark contrast to the bombed-out Korean schools in the news, and peace—which, when you came late to school in the waxing heat of a summer morning, was already echoing in psalmodic tones from all the classroom windows—daily thwarted the dreams of the pupils who hoped to arrive one day to find a smoking heap of rubble. The peace was filled with the literature of war; history was taught without textbooks, the one-armed teachers, free to extemporize, spoke with unconcealed enthusiasm of the initial German gains on the Eastern front and the extraordinary discipline that had made them possible, and in the afternoons in the movie theaters showing *Storm over Asia*, the crowd scenes elicited frenetic yelling from the young audience; the mustachioed Stalin portraits had already vanished from the walls, the pictures of the man who'd put an end to the Blitzkriegs, who'd brought the peace; peace was prose, but war was an ancient form of poetry that lay beyond all borders, in unseen lands, in the distance. — In the prose of that existence all the one-armed teachers had just one goal, one sacrament, knew just one religion, which they championed with all the means at their disposal, persuasion and seduction, testimony and censorship: *peace education*; at last, for the first time ever, all the teachers' aggression against their pupils' budding autonomy was animated by a righteous goal, it served the cause of peace; the violence of demagogy, the culture of denunciation, all the subjugation inflicted on the next generation at last had a humanistic ethos. But what an effect this had; deluged with proclamations of peace, the kids banded together in the schoolyards to wage new, childish wars; the especially hollow-cheeked, especially scruffy children from families repatriated from the east, who lived in the barracks of the former prison camp behind the gutted HASAG munitions factories, were the foreigners who had to be battled; plans for these campaigns were forged during recess in the cinder yard, and there were heaps of volunteers; the identity of the enemy was constantly updated; initially, a word picked up from the grown-ups, the repatriates had the look of *Buchenwald*, but soon they were *Korea*; in the afternoons veritable wars were fought with slung stones in the ruins of the HASAG, entrenched battles over empty, still-standing factory halls lasted until darkness fell, and in the underground system of sprawling, complex tunnels that honeycombed the terrain, bitter skirmishes raged over every branch of the passageways, for to control this system—a labyrinth from which several slingshot-armed schoolboys never returned—was to rule the ruins' entire expanse.

The peculiar thing was that this generation born in the war—the generation whose first three or four years the war had bound up and surrounded with the texture of maternal warmth…the generation that, years after the war's end, was still conspiring to perpetuate the state of war in its games (the unparalleled extreme of maternal protectiveness in the years of actual war had left the generation with an instinctive, unconscious tenderness for that very state)—seemed, in the subsequent decades of peace, to *vanish* into an indecipherable meaning, into the stillness of peace, into the fractures of peace. — Where have they gone, those whose names escape me no matter how I rack my brain, how many faces, vanished in the crowd, have I already passed by without a reunion. — I recall my alarm at nearly recognizing a face during the process of admission into prison, between property room, showers, crab lice, and haircuts, when—about to get my obligatory shots from the doctor, the dark-uniformed, booted *Frau Major*—amid the general cattle-to-the-slaughter anxiety, I was stricken by panic because one of the *old cons* acting as a medic had addressed me: Hey, haven't we met somewhere. — I recognized the ironically smiling, young-seeming face, but I didn't know where from, and instantly I felt that he was a former classmate of mine. — Up to '59 you were an apprentice at the training workshop in M., he explained, and I was an instructor there. — So it wasn't just the schoolboys who'd vanished from the scene. — Peace had descended on the world with a massive, irreversibly advancing rift, and the schoolboys had sought a life on the side of the riven world proclaimed to be that of the *robbers*; the attributes that this side ascribed to the other, chaos, gangsterism, lust for war, exerted a magical attraction over the generation whose backbone had been broken for the sake of peace. — I never saw them again, the boys of my cohort; for all the songs sung at each morning's flag ceremony, none of them had been born to be fighters for peace…they had vanished into the state's institutions, faceless, their genius utterly lost. And had those who'd crossed the border also vanished without a trace, or was there a storehouse of memories that I hadn't yet discovered…I was left behind, with a brain palpably burdened by the leaden weight of embedded meanings…I'd spent the first few days in prison afraid of running into one of them, and then it seemed incredible that I hadn't run into any of them, until finally I hit on the idea that I alone had been left behind in order to end up here…in the long sleepless nights in the cell the word *camp* had lodged itself in my mind, it had seemed possible to grasp the word in all its awful meanings…now it was possible no longer…I recalled how during my arrest, during the entire, endless-seeming drive to the prison, I'd been filled to bursting with screams that couldn't escape, that couldn't be shaped into words, that stayed inside me, an undeniable madness that I held back only by storing it away inside…when, later on, countless times, I replayed in my mind the path that took me from the house to the van and that marked the onset of mental darkness, I found the words of that scream, and I screamed once again, silent screams whose meaning I failed to grasp, yet as fierce as though they could name all the reasons for my possible salvation, it's clear to see, I screamed, it's more than clear, and it's enough, I was born in the *camp of peace*, as one of the few of the many…and in another part of my mind was the lurid memory of the sidewalk outside my house rearing up, torn from its bed, and covering the entire street with its debris; at the same time, from all over town, the bomb hits stood out audibly against the general infernal din into which the atmosphere was transformed; at the same time the water of the burst mains boomed, shooting up from the rupturing streets, fountains blindingly white amid inextricably merging conflagrations.

He saw that where the branches of the riven nightshade tree reached over the wall into the schoolyard, they had lost their leaves and withered as though in revulsion. — In those nights in prison, how could he have forgotten that safest point of departure for the escape maneuvers of his early youth, in the shadow of the wall. From here those in the know could vanish from the school grounds during recess, here the wall had an unused, forbidden door, hidden by the proliferating underbrush beneath the nightshade tree and seemingly impassable. It was chained and padlocked, but one of the older boys had a secret key, and sometimes, unnoticed by the school staff, the padlock was found open, as though by magic. If his prison fantasies had taken him to that spot beyond the wall, maybe he would have seen his comrades again, have rediscovered their faces, unrecognizably smeared with the juice of the nightshade, and they wouldn't have slipped from his mind…he'd have found help for his escape; from here a quiet, overgrown path led to the nearby forest. But no, he always passed by the ruins, which by the end of his time at school were already strangely depopulated, and each day closed with a chastened return, inconceivable derealizations lurked everywhere, the language of his thoughts proved helpless against them, utterly inadequate, only in those wanderings did it happen that a person suppressed within him, his truth-person, he suspected, gained the upper hand with the paralyzing refusal to acknowledge that the objects he encountered were the world; more and more he felt the urge to seek out that truth-person within him, but bitterly he grasped that that person—though seeming to divest the derealized world of its substance and revealing it as porous, threadbare, transparent—kept secret the truth that ought to have appeared behind it.

He left town, heading southeast, and roamed dense woods, climbing the hill behind the former HASAG prison camp; the reinforced concrete pillars of the camp's erstwhile fence, angled inward at the top, had been linked anew with wire mesh, marking one side of the sports and parade ground for the school's summer games (which he'd refused to take part in last time); from here he could see the black ruins of the *Progress* lignite mine, which, though undamaged in the war, had soon afterwards been shut down and half demolished due to dwindling deposits; now craggy, menacing building fragments loomed between the fields, seeming at the point of collapsing entirely; part of the mine, the former workshop, now functioned as the training facility and the plant's vocational school; also surrounded by a wire fence, it was the place he'd be banished to after graduation. — My *development* was already predetermined; a pole rose from the middle of the fenced-in yard, and from it dangled the same unmoving blue flag as from the pole in the center of the school's cinder yard.

A haze hung above it, and the road that connected the town to several nearby villages and intersected the path at this point—up here on the hill it was worn to a gravel track with mere islands of asphalt—descended in wide curves into a haze in which the meadows, the blue-green potato fields, and the sky seemed to converge. But even now the disenchantments wrought by sharper sunlight refused to loosen their grip on his memory; the receding planes of the croplands, the sky drawing close to the meadows, seemed to lack the southerly atmosphere he'd hoped for, and it seemed to be too late. In truth, though, when he wasn't too weary, when he could believe in the figure he'd rediscovered inside himself, when he didn't regard it as annihilated along with reality…for instance in the moment of his transformation into a Greek god, the tracts of the sky could be trodden; when he set foot there, the sky rose to immense heights behind him, over the ruins' black upward-pointing fingers. There lay the azure of memory; when the schoolboy managed to return to the youth of German Hellenism, he'd been close to that lofty remoteness…azure; as though to save him from falling, it descended again, flooding the receding valleys far and wide, on the way to Bordeaux, filled with fire, the fiery gates open to stride through. But already he'd gone on too long, continued too far along the old way; ahead of him, at the end of the road, in front of the dark strip of woodland, when his gaze briefly penetrated the haze of the enfolded sky that mingled with the blue-green light of the potato fields, the clearest image on the evening plain was an all-too-familiar, hostile village where the medieval steeple of a Catholic church loomed.

Each of the schoolboy's forays ended at the crest of that knoll where the world seemed to divide: into youth and old age, genius and barbarism, a past that had an existence and a future in which existence vanished in the absence of place. Behind all the derealizations, the future could not be discerned, and I wandered homeward through woods plowed by gigantic bomb craters, eerie in the onset of twilight; the student of the world returned perturbed to the town whose seams every stone filled, unshakably set in its peace, without a single gap.

The infallible instinct for identifying voices and noises (the only way to discern the value, the stability of the peace) was something he'd quickly learned in those nights in the detention cell. Only once, toward the end of his term, did he seem to mistake a cry; a commotion that broke out just outside the cell door, at dusk with a curfew already in effect, presented the precise image of a scene in which every sound, placed in relation to the prison's corridors, instantly *visualized* the matching detail with perfect transparency.

After minutes of unintelligible cries echoing from the disorienting remoteness of a distant cell, I heard rapid steps, several people rushing down the corridors; near our cell the steps escalated to a loud, furious run, and I heard the slapping blows of rubber truncheons clenched in several fists raining down on a person, a prisoner who responded by bursting into shrieks that echoed through the building, so loud and shrill that the inmates in my cell started up out of their sleep; what unmistakably followed, clearly indicated by a few intelligible words amid the yells, was the rumble and clatter as a person was pushed down the steep stairs to the ground floor; then the steps of the others rushing down the stairs, and again voices giving commands mixed with obscenities (the identity of the guards' voices obscured by their bellowing); then, after a moment's silence, feet dragging and shuffling, a cell door unlocking with a rattle on the ground floor where the solitary cells were, a body being dumped into a room, the crash of the door as it was closed and locked, the agitated murmur of the guards moving off.

Either following that scene or in an intense dream that night he thought he recognized the victim's face from his screams (rather than curses or cries for help, the prisoner had uttered words that vividly evoked his appearance); he must have heard that man's screams at some earlier point (after a short time in prison, before habituation has its leveling effect, one learns that even screams can have an individual note), those screams had a face that he clearly remembered; if he wasn't mistaken, he knew it, blood-smeared though it was; he knew the parted lips' pain-twisted shape, the opening between the rows of teeth, hung with red strands of saliva, but it was impossible to recall the person with that familiar face… toward morning he thought he realized his mistake; what stained that face wasn't blood, it was the dark red juice of the nightshade berries pilfered at recess.

The vanished figures, the great horde of all those I knew, whom I had in my head, in whose heads I was, were left in limbo; here, too, they were nowhere to be found. If it was I, still in the process of learning the world, if it was I alone who embodied what I'd claimed about everyone: that peace seemed unlearnable for our generation…then it was I who'd been left behind, and my generation had entered into peace, I alone had vanished, my face beyond recall for the peace-dwellers.

He had an intuition that, in the world he beheld riven by errors and schisms, erring was an essential form of existence, that his barely solid I, moving from aberration to aberration, must face the world's derealizations by *not* lending them mental reality…even his imprisoned body, which experienced prison as the most intense bond to a system whose aim was the *safeguarding of peace*, could be apprehended only by means of the papers waiting on the kitchen table, but those papers pertained to someone else, a hollow body that gravity had ensnared in the system's safeguards, that body, that mere shell that their predictable methods had taken as a reference point—it amazed him that fingerprinting and olfactory samples, photos, roll calls, and cell lights switched on in the night had even been able to establish his presence—that body had lost something in the shattering sounds of its latest sensory impression, its mental visage had vanished behind veils the color of blood.

Where are you, he cried, and for all his effort it was a soundless cry, the voice of a sleeper at the end of his sleep, where are you, irretrievable ones… in the exhausted sleep following a collapse, while listening to a sacred chant in which he discovered the Hebrew word for peace; he'd heard it was the everyday greeting of the people who, one historical moment ago, had nearly perished in his country's *camps*… where are you, comrades of my youth, a cry emerging from a sleep that had made him miss the midday train to the district capital, delaying by one dangerous day the registration with the authorities set for today; the inevitable, rapidly escalating conclusions the authorities would draw could not be allowed into his brain, lest total paralysis ensue. — When he bolted down the stairs, papers hidden in his pocket, passing the staring neighbors without a word in theatrical haste—in the hope of making himself *visible*—intent on reaching the train station, though he knew he'd never make the

105

train to the district capital…the midday light was gone, only certain glimmers here and there in the sky, beneath which the heavy smudges of the next rain hung, gave a hint of the flames roaring over the rims of braziers, one last time, the tattered gray cloud cover was already closing over them…poetic symbols had to serve as evidence for the renewed loss of reality.

Or are you the ones who vanished there, you who are blind to my body's empty shell…are you vanishing into the mists, abducted by a gigantic mountain, are you the beings dwelling in that massif's civilization of huts, are you the ones living in the semicircular structures made from animal dung…and what do you live on, are you living well in your immeasurable realm of the dead… your realm is dead and lost to the world.

I'd been mistaken; there was no precipice the huts adhered to, the whole thing was one single mountain of dwellings, the shape of that world had been erected in the image of the first hut built on Asiatic soil once upon a time. But when those huts had densely covered the whole land, all the way to its shores, they started building upward, a third layer atop the second, and so on, until that prodigious oval peak took form, a gigantic building in the same *necessary* shape as each of its component parts. A path taken from the ground to a dwelling in the middle of, let's say, the 150th floor would inevitably pass through all the occupied interiors of the stacked and nested huts; it was hard to grasp the advanced culture of coexistence those circumstances dictated; in that world a single injustice could become the epicenter of a quake, spreading in all directions and bringing down the entire realm…each individual in that world had to possess a single, open I, nothing was hidden, and nothing could be allowed to be hidden…the light's harsh rays in the high mountains' thin air had slowly dried the building material and fused all details into one whole; it must have taken eons for that world to achieve perfection. Mild red mists enveloped the whole thing, and gradually it vanished, soon all I saw was the yellow-green silhouette of the egg-shaped tip looming from the clouds, seemingly borne off by invisible wings.

My final recollection—as vivid as though my remote mind were receiving proof of a reality—was of the warm, vegetative vapors that flowed from all the building's openings, so warm and strong that the air currents over the ice-blue water of the shorelessly sprawling mountain lake were set in motion, propelling the sailing ships away in all directions; no one reached that legendary culture that took in prisoners no longer.

(On my way to the train station it occurred to me that in passing I'd actually glimpsed a white piece of paper behind the grille of my mailbox. I went back and retrieved it; it was a summons from the police.)

III

THE STOKER

If you open your mouth, you must go on.
If you've opened your mouth, you can repeat.
Helmut Heißenbüttel

Filled with anxiety, on the 20th of February, the stoker H., his night shift just finished, boarded the factory bus waiting at the entrance to the small, outlying unit of the operation where he worked; behind him the driver instantly closed the doors with that familiar hiss and, before the stoker could find a seat, launched into his habitual maneuvers, backing and swiveling on the narrow, barely lit road between the railway embankment and slopes plunging deep into old lignite strip mines with a nonchalant routine that made a mockery of safety precautions. The heat inside the bus, saturated with the conglomerated effluvia of the work gang that it had spat out at the factory entrance, made the stoker momentarily forget his destination; touched with wonder by these smells—left intact by a smidgen of soap—of featherbeds wrestled with all night, he sat cushioned by his seat, tracing the top notes of the fragrance, perfumes shed by the three or four secretaries or coffee ladies who arrived at this early hour; usually those scents were like stray hints of phosphorescent rouge vanishing in a mass of dark, blurred faces, but today they seemed to float above the bed smell with special vigor and variety; this was a moment when the craving for a cigarette always overcame him, making him flout the no-smoking signs; behind the back of the driver, whose silence in the face of this daily transgression suggested tacit consent, he started one of those expensive filtered cigarettes he saved especially for such moments.

Heading home after the night shift, the stoker was generally the sole passenger as the bus made its trip back to town, since his unit worked on the single-shift system; each morning, enclosed in the vehicle's warm interior, he felt liberated as he left the small complex, the one located farthest from operation headquarters, where he passed the night alone but for an ancient porter who rarely ventured from his gatehouse, the loneliest imaginable graveyard shift worker in surroundings he described with the antiquated word *spectral*. It didn't bother the stoker at all, the way the driver took the bus at breakneck speed over enormous potholes, so deep and wide that the bus seemed to lift off for moments at a time—fortunately, it was an extremely robust Russian model, but with its snub, tall body atop the spring-loaded chassis, it lurched all the more madly—while the poplars along the dropoff into the mining pit flew past like fog and the headlights glared into the darkness, there being no streetlights out in this wasteland; the stoker was used to this morning race against the vigilance of the railroad crossing guard, knowing that just minutes after the workers got off the bus and he got on, the boom gates of the railroad crossing where the road ended—next to an abandoned train station that years ago had served a village since fallen prey to the strip mines—would close to let several trains pass in succession; already the old station's blind windows were gleaming in the headlights, the bus swerved with dizzying speed around the building; too late; as so often, it stopped with a jolt at the lowered boom gates.

The driver let out a curse, loud but resigned, turning on the radio just as the 5:30 news began; too late; at 5:30 sharp the gates had to be closed. Now, as so often, he'd be twenty minutes late delivering the next load of passengers, the newly built foundry's office staff, to their workplace. Turning his head halfway around he asked: Anyone have a cigarette for me. — The stoker went up and offered the driver a filtered cigarette, reason enough to treat himself to another one. — Can you take me as far as the foundry, he asked as he gave the driver a light, I want to pick up my year-end bonus. — Oh, the year-end bonus… the stoker couldn't fail to hear the driver's spiteful sarcasm. I get it. But today I've got to make a little detour, he added, well, let's get a move on, then… — He was practically yelling; at that very moment the first freight train was thundering past. — A detour… the stoker echoed; taking his seat again, he hoped the detour would mean that he wouldn't have to greet his superiors, who got on at the entrance to the main factory, that today they'd take a different bus to the foundry, sparing him from sitting next to the factory's chief heating engineer whose pleasant small talk would make it virtually impossible to dispute the year-end bonus with the friendly old man once they got to the office.

As in years past, the workers in the support divisions were the last to receive their year-end bonuses; the scuttlebutt among the stokers—nothing could persuade them otherwise—was that they had to divvy up whatever was left over; H. perfectly understood the driver's sarcasm: by the time the stokers were paid their share, the other divisions' festering dissatisfaction over the amounts received had already filtered through. Over the past two or three years those amounts had continually decreased, though the annual plan targets kept rising and the plans kept being fulfilled: gone were the days when, in February of the new planning year, you'd look back triumphantly at the past year with a pocket full of cash far exceeding a month's wages, and with a beneficent smile you'd set down the obligatory two percent thereof in the account for the union's solidarity fund, or even decide to increase your donation. All that was a thing of the past; everyone knew that for the past several years the plans were being fulfilled only by working more and more overtime, that the targets kept being raised by planners apparently unconcerned with how they'd be met, while, for some reason, the year-end bonuses failed to keep pace.

A third, unending freight train trundled through the darkness, gradually picking up speed; the lampposts and buildings outside were enveloped by tatters of vapor descending and whirling back up again; a fine, indistinct rain seemed to dance through the cones of light; at last the boom gates rose and the bus driver coaxed one first, fizzling howl from the switched-off engine. At that very moment the stoker thought he heard an inexplicable grinding crunch behind him; again the engine revved up and died, and the driver, judging by whimpering sounds softer than the pop music on the radio, made cautious attempts to start it up again; right in the pause between two songs the stoker heard another crunch behind him, grinding hideously now, unquestionably behind his back, so loud that later he'd couldn't have said whether the driver oughtn't to have heard it as well; just as the bus started up with a roar, the stoker clearly felt a dull, soft impact behind him, noticeable only as a jolt to the bus floor; he looked around in alarm, but saw nothing but the seat backs and aluminum bars of the bus's empty interior. In the evident absence of any threat, his shudder died away, but in searching for an explanation, he suddenly seemed to realize: it was unmistakable, preternaturally clear, that what he'd heard was the loud—in his ears, deafening—grinding of teeth. That thought made him spin around again, but there was nothing in the empty bus to indicate so awful a noise.

We've got to pick someone up, there's another guy who wants his bonus, the driver shot that belated explanation over his shoulder, and as a huddle of barely familiar farmsteads appeared, the bus, having traveled tortuous, virtually unnegotiable stretches of road between villages and fields, came to a stop at a highway ramp and the front and back doors opened with the familiar hiss of compressed air. The light of a streetlamp struggled through the morning darkness that only seemed to grow denser, the howl of a storm drowned out the idling motor, snowflakes sped through the swaying spaces of light outside the doors of the quivering bus in what seemed a furious attempt to infiltrate the warm interior. To H.'s mind, the driver was waiting far too long for the other passenger who was apparently supposed to show up; damp cold flooded the bus, and H. listened as the storm seemed to grow stronger, possibly portending winter's late return, a nasty cold snap that would call for working weekends again; he heard the storm whipping at trees and loose fence pickets, the door panels rattling, the groaning and scratching along the sheet-metal exterior that often seemed to mask the infinitely weary work of human strides; at last, with mute abruptness, the driver slammed the doors shut. At that moment, in one plexiglass pane of the folding back door, the stoker saw an old, wrinkled, yellow face with bulging eyes pressed outside against the pane, the cry of a gaping mouth broke off inaudibly; leaping forward, the bus wiped that face away; the stoker thought he'd glimpsed a likewise yellow, scrawny human hand clutching vainly for a hold, but also instantly falling behind.

Later, the stoker could have sworn that he'd leapt up and rushed to the back window, but saw nothing but snow whirling over the road as it vanished into the darkness; that he'd sat back down again and, staring at the driver's utterly unperturbed back, tried for a long time to shake off his horror. No doubt about it, his sleep-deprived nerves had conjured up hallucinations; fortunately the driver didn't seem to have noticed the way he'd jumped up like a crazy person…but what if he *hadn't* jumped up, what if even that had been a hallucination.

It's no good, we're not going to make it, no way, the driver yelled, that damn railroad crossing… — Now, on the level highway surface, he seemed to press the gas pedal down to the floor, and at full tilt the vehicle lapsed into a steady sort of song, alarming the stoker; the headlights of oncoming cars flashed like lightning through the bus's carapace as it raced toward a bright streak visible at last over smokestacks, the town of M. looming on the horizon. Fear suffused the stoker's limbs; the recent snow flurries must have left the asphalt damp and slippery, but the driver's self-confidence seemed to keep growing; once, overtaking a freight train, the bus grazed the branches of the cherry trees on the left-hand shoulder, not with the usual scraping sound but with a lashing crack that the driver acknowledged with a loud laugh. Fortunately, they could already see the outskirts of M., and the hair-raising pace had to be curbed. — Now the stoker realized that he was huddled in his seat dissolved in floods of sweat, as though he'd lost his senses; he barely registered the bus's erratic journey through M.'s labyrinthine streets or the driver's curses as detour signs kept looming; he'd barely noticed that they'd stopped for a few seconds by a front garden in the neighborhood of

Z., that the bus doors had swung open again, nor could
he have said whether anyone had gotten on or off. Later
he thought it possible that during that stop he'd heard
behind him the shy greeting of a porter, an old man of his
acquaintance who, due to his infirmity, had had himself
transferred from the stoker's squalid unit to a different
job. Had the old man read some kind of horror in the
stoker's face, was that why his greeting had come out
so shyly… The stoker shook his head at himself and sat
up straight in his seat; the singed filter of his cigarette
lay at his feet and he felt a painful burn-blister on his
index finger. Maybe he'd just imagined the old porter's
good morning, due to all the times the frail voice had
greeted him when the bus stopped at that garden gate
in Z. Could it be that sleep had overcome him on that
careening bus ride… The stoker was too exhausted even
to glance back and satisfy himself whether anyone was
sitting behind him, whether anyone had gotten on or off.
At last the bus stopped next to a sullenly waiting crowd
outside the gate of the main factory in M., the doors
opened, and with a hubbub of voices the stampede for
the inadequate number of seats began.

He'd been mistaken, then, in assuming that the
managers wouldn't be taking this bus out to the foundry.
The seat beside him was free; in a moment the chief
heating engineer, the *foreman*, would get on, and the
stoker could only hope that a younger worker would be
quick enough to grab the seat first. He sat up straight
again and glanced at the glass pane beside his head, but

it was already gray outside, and the window barely showed his reflection, all he could make out, in a patch of sallow yellow, was the black of the deep furrows reaching toward the corners of his mouth; his skin's yellow hue alarmed him, my God, he thought, that's a madman's face leering at me. And what possessed me to go all the way out there just for that bonus. — He knew it was the managers' duty to bring him his bonus at his work station. But he also knew just why he was going there, and in fact it was customary for the stokers who worked scattered throughout the operation to pick up their bonuses themselves…as if the fastest ones would get the biggest bonuses, H. thought scornfully. Anyway, they'd just have sent a secretary, and what good was a secretary when the point was to use the expected solidarity donation as a way to send a message. — The doors of the packed bus had finally closed, and he was sure that the gray-haired foreman hadn't gotten on; his face, always cheerful even at that early hour, was nowhere to be seen. The old foreman was unpopular among the younger bosses; secret turf battles were supposedly raging among the leadership of the heating department, but so far the old man had held his ground, though he was regarded as phlegmatic, indeed unreliable, tending to take the stokers' side in disputes; when there were technical problems and everyone looked in his direction as though expecting a miracle, he'd declare with eyes half-shut: Now listen, you know I actually retired ages ago… but H. knew that appearances were deceptive and the old man with all his experience would be hard for the unit to replace. — Morning—this greeting, both vowels precisely stressed, met him from the side, together with a whiff of stale alcohol that made him flinch. Next to him sat a young, black-haired man, one of the several hundred Arab coworkers who'd been assigned to the factory over a year ago, all reputed to be *lazy bums*; indeed, so far the operation seemed to have failed miserably at getting the young North Africans to come to work five days a week; they were unable to adapt to starting at the set time of 5:30 AM, and it seemed impossible to convince them that the assigned tasks genuinely needed to be performed. When the stoker's colleagues had predicted as much, he'd taken it for malicious cliches: They're all lazy dogs, they'll never learn to work. When those camel drivers come, we'll have to do their work on top of our own. — H., who'd defended the North Africans, discovered that it was true, they had no intention of sweeping the control rooms or storerooms several times a shift; he admired the discipline with which, generally right after breakfast, as though by mutual agreement, they vanished without a trace. — It tasted real good last night, that German beer, his black-haired neighbor explained, Germany's hard to take, lots of work, no hospitality, but beer is good, very good, and that bonus yesterday, year-end bonus, lots of money, lots of beer... — Solidarity, thought the stoker, not much year-end bonus, not much solidarity... — He felt weariness in all his limbs, his anxiety at what awaited him had turned to leaden weariness. — I could have gone to bed ages ago, surely they'd have brought me the damn bonus to my apartment in the afternoon... in the afternoon, when, having just gotten up, he'd still have been tired enough to spinelessly pay the donation they demanded. He sensed that his courage to create a scandal—as he called his plan—had vanished, because he knew it wouldn't alter his situation. All he wanted to do was call attention to the working conditions in Plant 6, or rather, less sweepingly, to his own problems in that remote unit, but that would require an incident that would communicate his case to the offices with broader remits; he felt that the Energy Department, i.e. his immediate superiors, occupied too low a level within the operation's management pyramid. The most effective incident would be one with a certain political edge, though of course it mustn't have legal consequences. For good reason, he was reluctant to consider a venerable method that, given the general labor shortage, had often proven effective. That method consisted of presenting the managers with a choice at the end of the heating season: Either you move me out of the Plant 6 boiler room, or this was my last winter here, you'll have to face it, I'm quitting. You've got time till next fall to find a new man for this unit. — Word had gotten out that the old, officially retired foreman, with whom it had proved possible to negotiate that way, was going to leave the operation that spring; the new foreman, who was already in charge of many things, definitely including staff issues, wouldn't know the routine: H.'s boiler room is in Plant 6; after spending the summer with a good job in the foundry—almost too much of a good thing, certainly enough to exonerate the guy—in the fall H. goes back to Plant 6, where everyone knows he's the best man, the one who's known that boiler room the longest. — After just a few weeks on the job the new foreman was already known for his hard line, risking staff turnover rather than compromising, and taking a formal tone with people: If you don't want to work in Plant 6, Mr. H., you're free to give notice… — But H. knew that there were other options in this operation, there were vacancies—necessitating difficult workarounds—at the switching stations in the units supplied with long-distance steam heat from the power plant, clean, quiet workstations where you had an unusual amount of freedom. The thing was to use the tiny remnant of wiggle room and call those vacancies to the old man's attention, orchestrate the *scandal* so that the old man would say: Get this guy out of here, he's gone psycho over in Plant 6, let him recuperate in Long-Distance Steam… Not a bad plan, the way H. figured it, but he knew it would become harder and harder to carry out; the new foreman's first, major accomplishment would be to finally provide Plant 6 with a stable, reliable stoking crew. — There would be even less point in confronting the new foreman: Listen, sir, I'm speaking to you as the author that I am outside my working hours, as a side job, if you will; I'm requesting support for a project, an artistic project, art is part of life as well. For this project, this book, you can call it a novel, I need two years' time, the only way I can pull it off is if I'm transferred to Long-Distance Steam; I don't mind taking a financial loss, I'm not asking for much, and in Long-Distance Steam I can do my work every day, on schedule, I know it's not much work, but that's just the thing... — The very first sentences made him feel how inescapably absurd such a speech would be, his request struck him as overblown, indeed utterly over the top, he sensed its out-of-control theatricality, but he knew that as long as he stuck to the language of the operation and the new foreman, the language of submission to the interests of the operation, he'd leave them every option to refuse his request; indeed that he would be showing them the simplest way to deal with the problem, namely with a refusal. But what language should he, the stoker, use to speak to his boss; he was the stoker, any other language, were it even conceivable, would be the implausible language of a nonexistent character, the language of a character in a novel... — Very interesting to hear that you're active as a People's artist in your spare time, the new foreman replied, that's worth encouraging, a type of meaningful leisure activity, and naturally it has our full support—I don't need to remind you of the ideals of Bitterfeld. The Bitterfeld conference made it clear what talents are emerging from the ranks of the workers, but it's certainly interesting to see that even in our own ranks we're reaping the benefits of People's art...of course we're aware of the situation in Plant 6, but of course you're equally aware of it, the Plant 6 staff situation, that is. As you've correctly noted, our most pressing task is to solve those problems, and, as always, we expect your cooperation, your total commitment, so naturally no allowances can be made for your…journal, did you call it. As you know, that's hardly feasible, but on the other hand there's no question that we'd be interested in a journal documenting problem-solving in our current precarious situation from the perspective of someone on the ground, especially since it could have a stimulating effect when read aloud at meetings… —

Had he been drinking last night too… He was roused by his neighbor's voice; the North African colleague next to him grinned; he was asking because the stoker was taking such a late bus. — I was working the night shift, the stoker replied. — Oh, right, night shift. Night shift no good, lots of work, not much money. — How late is it, anyway, H. asked, it seemed to be broad daylight already, and the bus was rolling down the ramp to the foundry grounds. The Arab showed him his watch, it was 7:30 AM, which meant that in some mysterious fashion—probably in my sleep, he thought derisively—the stoker had wound up on the first of the buses that ran hourly between the different units of the operation carrying workers who liaised in various ways between the different, widely dispersed plants; in other words, through some complex chain of circumstances he must have missed all the morning shuttle buses, including the last bus for the office workers.

Better late than never, the old foreman greeted him as he entered the brightly lit office of the Energy Department, housed in an almost overheated shed pervaded by the smell of freshly brewed coffee. — He was probably home having breakfast, said the secretary, and now he can join us for a cup of coffee. — The stoker, vulnerable to excesses of friendliness in his sleep-deprived state, wondered whether to refuse. It was the first time he'd been offered coffee here; his year-end bonus wouldn't amount to much, he knew what his other two coworkers from Plant 6 had gotten, a good hundred marks less than the previous year; he'd never been one for picking a fight, a cup of coffee and he'd be completely mollified. — Why not, said the new foreman, sitting at a nearby desk, this day calls for a bit of a celebration. — Evidently his assent was required for the exceptional occurrence that now ensued. Everyone knew about the bottle of brandy that the old foreman kept in the cabinet, but no one had ever set eyes on it. — You've knocked off work already, said the secretary, and as for us, you won't tell tales. — At a smile from the old foreman, she'd gotten up and set four glasses on the table; the stoker, a coffee already in front of him, heard the dainty tinkle as the brandy filled the glasses. — But first, let's get down to work, the old foreman said, laying the bonus list on the table, ultimately this is the only day when we get to draw these fine, but essential, distinctions. — At one glance the stoker saw that his bonus came to fifty marks more than his two colleagues at Plant 6 had gotten. In the proper column he signed off on the receipt of a 650-mark bonus, noticed that he was the last to sign the list, and tucked the envelope in his pocket without counting the money. — The secretary, noticing, gave an approving nod, It's all right, we double-checked. — The stoker, unable to hide his fingers' trembling from that gaze, had already drunk from his cup (it took just an automatic reflex, a miniscule lapse of the executive function to make his hand reach for the cup and lift it to his lips) and the coffee had corrupted him; the stoker lived in a society where you couldn't even accept a cup of coffee without being bought and paid for; the coffee was hot and black (the stoker, in one last senseless burst of defiance, had refused cream and sugar) and did him a world of good; inside he was parched and drained from the long night, while outside he felt the unpleasant touch of moisture, finally warming, from clothes soaked by the February rain; he had to reassure himself that it wasn't sweat, or his unrested body's foul exhalations, it was rain that had run down the back of his neck, he sat wrapped in its musty mantle. Unprompted, he reached for the brandy glass and drank—seize the chance to act like a lout, the idea came to him like a deliverance—it was a Romanian brandy, a sweet, cough-inducing sort; he'd swallowed too timidly and felt the shock of the drink in his throat, not his stomach; after hawking pathetically he had to take a swig of coffee; the glass he'd set down still held half an inch of liquid that had dribbled back from his feebly parted lips; he was all too keenly aware of a large drop in the stubble on his chin, but didn't dare to wipe it with the back of his hand, corrupted as he was; he hadn't shaved in three days and probably looked like a hoodlum, sitting there with damp temples and nostrils. — How's it taste, asked the secretary, hand already back on the bottle. — Night shift… the stoker gasped in explanation, the word, barely intelligible, merely transformed the burning in his throat into a wheeze. — Have another one, man, the old foreman said calmly; though perhaps without intent, his voice was just as corrupting as the fact that the stoker wasn't being told to go to hell, H. glanced up at the new foreman's eyes, keenly observant over his smile, and past them, so as not to see the secretary pour him a fresh brandy. — Yeah, well, thanks for the bonus… he said, cowed, fortunately ignored by the old foreman, who launched in on a speech. — Actually, I've already vanished, he said, and the person sitting here with you is nothing but my ghost. Yesterday was my last day on the job, you know I've been retired for ages already…heck, actually I'm already dead, and this bonus was my last official piece of business, I've risen from the grave for a while to tell you, the last guy, a day late already…to tell you that from this day on the fellow you see there is your new boss, you know the man, from now on he's in charge of all relevant issues et cetera, as a dead man all that's left me is the final duty, you know the routine…but first of all, before we forget, we want to drink to this moment. — And indeed, the glasses were raised and met in the middle, the stoker saw his shot glass, held in two fingers that no longer felt like his, join the other glasses with absurd assurance. To everyone's health, to my retirement, came the old foreman's voice. Cheers, came his own voice, confident again, human again; his sensation of himself returned only when he felt half the brandy wash over his tongue, tasting better now; he set the half-full glass within reach and finished off the suddenly cold coffee. He couldn't remember how he'd ended up in this room.

Had it been dark still when he got off the bus at the foundry grounds; toward the end it had turned chilly, as though the driver had switched off the heat too soon; in the chill all the passengers' limbs had been filled with life, without a trace of death, which alone could have fit intelligibly into the light of that memory; he'd smelled their morning smells, already stale-seeming—the hyper-trophied soap and perfume smells of the administrative workers—smelled them so intensely that they sapped his shaky inner life and the alcohol on his neighbor's breath triggered attacks of nausea, so that he had to tilt his head back and breathe deep, plagued by a ravenous craving for cigarette smoke, as though that alone could kill off the oppressive life of the body. Outside the plant entrance in the dark—definitely: in the dark—on the expanse of concrete lashed by rain and wind, he'd laboriously lit a cigarette, using up multiple matches, left behind all alone as everyone else ran off toward the plant to get out of the storm. He was last, which was cause enough for a thorough check by the policeman guarding the plant entrance: Where was he coming from, was it his shift

he was heading for, so late, an hour after work had begun, why didn't he have a foundry ID to legitimate his
presence. — Shed 7, Energy Department, picking up
my year-end bonus. — The bulky policeman, taller by
two heads, still staring at the stoker's ID in the light of
a lamp as though at some proof of all human filth, didn't
seem to hear a word. After inclining his head through the
feeble lamplight, almost to the point of physical contact
with the stoker, who, avoiding a collision with difficulty,
at last thought he saw a gleam of recognition in the
other's eyes, the officer rasped in a tone of command: Go
on. — Despite the inadequate light, the stoker glimpsed
a mouth full of half-rotten teeth; he grabbed his ID
and, already rain-soaked, unable to suppress his feelings
of revulsion, fled into the plant without duly acknowl-
edging the policeman's plaintive words: What about us,
are we the scum of the earth around here, where every
deadbeat, every shady specimen gets stuffed to the gills
with bonuses, everybody else, just not the likes of us...
— You're the ones who don't put your cards on the table,
moneywise, the stoker wasn't sure whether he'd actually
made that parting shot over his shoulder; for the first
time that morning he'd felt corrupted by the policeman's
complaint, which sounded plausible enough; he'd heard
that policemen didn't get year-end bonuses. He couldn't
muster any feeling of triumph in that regard; he put it
down to the solidarity problem that he was about to
confront. — Smoking, hiding the cigarette in his cupped
hand—smoking wasn't allowed on the factory grounds,

and besides, the rain was coming down harder—he'd covered the long distance to Shed 7, and despite the weather there were times when he found himself unable to quicken his pace.

The stoker drained the glass, unable to say whether it mightn't have been the third brandy already, alarmed at first to feel how even that small dose of alcohol impaired him, but then sensing a slight fuzziness to his thoughts that calmed him, as though it might soon serve him as an excuse; now he scoffed at himself for his hesitation en route to the shed, his notion of seeking refuge in the glass-fronted cafeteria, where light was already burning, and drinking a cup or two of coffee to muster his strength for the scene to follow. Behind the forest of exotic-looking plants that screened off the entire glass façade, in the still-dimmed light of the cafeteria—not open yet, but already serving a certain circle of insiders to whom he'd once belonged—the stoker watched the cleaning girls slip past, sedate and weary. A group of young workers lumbered past him from the changing rooms, dressed in protective quilted clothing and felt boots and making a beeline for the cafeteria entrance; as they strode through the circles of reddish light beneath the lamps their bright plastic helmets gleamed in the rain; it looked like the North Africans, and the stoker soon saw them hammering at the cafeteria door, prearranged knock signals. He felt cold moisture seeping through his shoes, transforming his socks into slimy foreign objects, sloughed off by the skin of his feet and forming bulges that pinched and chafed. For a moment he'd stopped to warm himself with the vivid memory of certain summer mornings—and they'd been cool mornings—when he'd sat at that same early hour in a cafeteria not yet filled with kitchen smells, where he'd sucked up the fragrance of the coffee and the smoke of cigarettes lit despite the smoking ban, hardly taking his eyes off the giggling girls in their short aprons who pushed around the softly humming floor polishers and bore the men's looks self-assuredly; hidden behind the green of the palms and rubber trees, those morning hours when he breathed in the weary voices of the young men and the giggling of the girls were hours of a forbidden splendor as promised by the thought of an African sun in whose light you return to your senses after a long, dreamlike escape. But behind the African forest of the glass front, the tables were now occupied by young Arab workers, drowning the previous day's alcohol in watery European coffee, their African sun gilded by solidarity, the dim neon tubes over their heads illuminating the complaisant spectacle of the girls with the polishing machines, transformed before their eyes into dancing houris. The stoker decided to report to the office first and go to the cafeteria afterward; he pictured himself—if everything went well and he managed to disrupt the mawkish ceremony of the bonus payment—striding upright out of the office, leaving a malevolent silence in his wake; if only he could seize back control of the time that had ambushed him and slipped away at some point in his sleep, he might still have enough leeway before his bus left to sit in the cafeteria and fight down the dread over his victory. No doubt about it, he thought it perfectly possible that the impending scandal might release him from all his ties to this factory, that today would be his last time on the premises of this factory that dominated the entire region.

Probably the factory dominated his entire fate, meaning that his arrival at the foundry, that time he'd gotten off the bus in the first light of dawn, might date back to a different day; the first work gangs were already marching into the cafeteria for breakfast, which was why he hadn't gone there himself. — He recalled that someone, one of the heads of the transport fleet, had gotten into an altercation with the bus driver; he couldn't make heads or tails of it, but he sensed how awkward the situation was, with that argument taking place in front of all the other passengers. The driver vehemently denied responsibility for some delay that his boss characterized as *practically spooky*, and suddenly the driver invoked the stoker as his witness, claiming, his voice rising to a scream, that the stoker could attest to some circumstance—the stoker hadn't caught the words describing it, nor could he imagine what it was about—because he himself had been involved, at which point everyone sitting or standing nearby gawked at the startled stoker. His mind was a complete blank, but to back up the driver, feigning quick-wittedness, he shouted to the front of the bus: That's right, I know all about it. — Which of course was completely wrong, a ridiculous remark, and to straighten things out he shouted: The driver's right, that's the way it was, I was there. — Which was probably just as wrong. But at that the driver took one hand from the steering wheel and stretched it out flat in front of his boss, as though the truth lay in the palm of his hand. The boss turned away from the driver with a dismissive wave and shot an ominous glance at the stoker. He was still haunted by that glance, wondering if it had held a threat and if that threat might have repercussions, as the bus arrived and he got off, noticing with alarm that it was already broad daylight, the snow flurries had long since turned to rain, the temperature seemed to be rising again. Before finally hurrying off to Shed 7—how long had he been keeping them waiting already—he gazed after the bus as it drove off, *definitely empty* now. There was no question, the driver he'd just defended must have been using him for some kind of devilry, no doubt about it, he'd fallen asleep in the bus and ridden the entire circuit, possibly more than once; the bus driver, grasping the situation, had let him sleep on so as to confirm his alibi for some nefarious purpose or other. Those thoughts plagued the stoker all the way to his destination; no doubt about it, you paid a price for working at a factory like this as long as he had. — In contrast to past years, he missed the scent of spring in this February rain, a scent that inspired him afresh at the start of each year to leave the factory forever. February was a good time to clear out, with that year-end bonus in your pocket; each year this was a time to reflect on the near-terror he felt at the prospect of leaving, days before the bonus was paid he'd already harbor the tremor that preceded that terror. — But today, entering Shed 7's long, practically overheated corridor, pausing for a moment to let the rain drip from his coat, soaked and sleep-deprived, he'd been beaten from the start; he'd entered the office corrupted by the shed's warm light, incapable of asserting himself in any way whatsoever.

Moving to light a cigarette, the stoker found just one lone match in his matchbox; it occurred to him that he'd used up almost all his matches in the storm outside the plant entrance; at the same time, he recalled the incredible suspicion with which the policeman at the gate had scrutinized him, he could still smell the horrendous stench exuded by the diseased teeth in the fat open-mouthed face that loomed so near, a smell that his nostrils seemed to have retained for an inexplicably long while, making a new, inexorable surge of nausea rise within him. Blanching, he felt sweat on his brow and the misgiving that what seemed to be spreading through the office was his own smell, his own awful taste in his mouth, the putrid smell of his own exhaustion and lack of sleep, he saw with horror that the moist hand holding his last match was trembling, it didn't seem to be his hand, it refused to obey him, letting the match burn out. At the tip of his cigarette a lighter flared, and the secretary exclaimed: Wrong… — The word pierced his very marrow, as though it transcended the immediate meaning he grasped far too late; the filter of his cigarette was already burning, he'd held it, instead of the tip, to the flame of the lighter offered by the old foreman, and it was spreading a new stench. — Aren't you feeling well, asked the secretary, clearly he looked too pathetic for anyone to laugh at his mishap. — I need another brandy, he mustered all his strength to gasp out. — I think we need a second man, the old foreman observed, for the boiler in Plant 6, at least for the night shift; this winter's over, but I'd definitely plan that in for the next heating season. — He didn't think, he went on to say after a frowning look at the stoker, who'd gone completely pale, that the work had gotten easier there the past few years, there were limits to the strain you could put on people, otherwise they'd start to think about quitting. This remark was aimed at the new foreman, who, the stoker saw through a veil that covered his eyes and cut off his thoughts, promptly made a note with his pencil. — A second man, said the stoker, that's just what we need… — He was too exhausted for irony, but he could see himself, in the few hours of respite left to him between bouts of shoveling coal—hours he'd spend huddled over his notebooks, despite his aching bones—harassed by the empty blather of some assistant they'd assigned him; to be sure, he'd gain time and energy, but he'd squander it daily in the most pointless possible way, chitchatting with a person who lacked any notion or understanding of the *duties of his second life*; finally he saw himself going to his boss to reject the assistant, demonstrating by example that the work in Plant 6 could perfectly well be shouldered by one person.

Before this he'd never *seen* himself in the boiler room of Plant 6, toiling in the catacomb of the old coal bunker… in his present state of mind he was suddenly able to see himself clearly. — His depictions of his life displayed an obvious obsessive streak…the search for justification; the ground on which that depicted life moved was a ground already primed, primed for explosions; in the effluvia and eddies over this ground, and in the hubbub that threatened to seal the stoker's vocal organs with an earthen coating, every random word he formed became an outcry, random sentences joined to produce expertise for incendiary acts. In the black dust clouds that shot up with each swing of the shovel and poured down again from the low ceiling, the stoker could barely be seen; only the moist spot of his face, mouth open and blood-red, swiveled momentarily with each twist of his torso into the blackened lightbulbs' red light. The challenge, a race against the dying of the fires in the boilers, was to shovel coal into a chest-high iron trolley in a cramped, poorly lit shaft, hampered by the lignite briquettes that kept sliding down, hampered by that iron wagon crowding your body; in no time the manometer needles fell to zero, and the fan heaters in the drafty factory halls, around whose gigantic free-standing forms the night frost had congealed in the atmosphere, would soon start producing cold air; the thermometer columns, upheld with the utmost effort at their already inadequate level, would instantly start to fall again, no doubt about it, the prescribed temperatures couldn't be maintained; when the work gangs poured into the factory in the morning their eyes would go straight to the thermometers, too cold, the stokers, those dogs, did they spend the night snoozing, did they spend it stoking their goddamn bodies with brandy, forgetting the factory halls; no one, not the engineers, not the workers, could be persuaded that the old boilers, installed decades ago, no longer sufficed to maintain the required working temperatures in below-freezing weather now that the factory, including this old section, was constantly expanding, now that, as per state decree, a new factory hall for the production of consumer goods had been built in special emergency shifts, ignoring the fact that new production halls called for new supply systems. For years the Energy Department's engineers had been knocking at the doors of the investment offices waving their calculations, but in vain. Those calculations were dismissed on the grounds that they were planning, they'd been planning for years, to supply this remote unit—standing on a narrow strip of land projecting out into the vastness of the exhausted strip mines and exposed to the iciest, most relentless winter winds—with long-distance steam heat from a nearby power plant, but the construction of the new, super-modern foundry had torpedoed the machine tool operation's budget. Each summer, after yet another heating season ridden out thanks to great exertions and a relatively mild winter, the grounds above the subterranean boiler rooms swarmed with technicians huddling around a host of measuring instruments and punting invisible but hotly debated coordinates back and forth through the morning sun; once again pipeline bridges and tunnels, as-yet-nonexistent foundations and fantastic steam reduction units were surveyed until, by fall at the latest, when the days had turned chilly and the technicians had disappeared again, there came the annual revelation that funding for the steam connection hadn't been freed up yet, and apologies were made at tight-lipped meetings: We too are at the mercy of the global market situation, things will have to go on as before for one more year. — Once again, mountains of coal descended on the stokers, coal of the most inferior sort, just barely good enough for the Plant 6 boiler room; once again, with shoulders pressed to the steel frame, the stokers thrust the screeching coal trolley over the boilers' flame-spewing filling shafts; once again they hurried through the winter cold with sweat-damp bodies to lug tons of stinking, smoking ash to the overflowing waste dumps; once again, every day, as temperatures sank inexorably to the stokers' horror, the indignant foremen marched from the factory halls to the boiler rooms, and the black, sweating, seething stokers raised their pokers to defend themselves against the incessant demands for heat, steam, heat, steam.

Why was he still putting up with this. Couldn't he escape the undeniable fascination of that basement with its flicker of embers and filth, couldn't he at least find easy work for low pay. Every winter, in the hopeless depths of January, when overtime and weekend shifts were the norm, there'd come a point when he'd swear to quit the factory that spring. — That was what he told himself, but then he'd have to leave town, in fact he'd have to leave the country whose small-town policemen had such a foul taste, spoiled by rotten teeth, eyes widening gigantic with suspicion and alarm, staring at the news that the *stoker* had suddenly refused to stoke and preferred to brood at a hidden writing desk over things impossible to monitor.

A sight he could not look away from, a sight that opened his mouth…though it was just as contrived as his character's monologues seemed when, from within one of his two lives, he tried to picture his semblance from the other…held him captive, gaping in the lurid light of a labyrinthine boiler room, amid the dance of gigantic blundering shadow-throngs performing senseless actions, he saw himself subject his body to furious Sisyphean labors; it was a body already exhausted and cracking, whose inner devastations erupted in unremitting coughing fits, black snot mingled with sudden nosebleeds, the savage sight of the shaggy, pesky shock of hair, soaked and filled with coal dust, the flushed brow that streamed sweat into eyes nearly blinded by burst veins, eyes that nonetheless saw him, in an attitude approaching frenzy amid a bombardment of sparks spraying from the seams of the soot-clogged boilers… he saw himself, alienated from all humanity, banished to an Industrial Age far removed from progress…he could almost see how the valve handwheels—their spindles overgrown by decades of boiler scale, requiring crowbars to budge them—were adorned by garlands of cast-iron flowers…one time he stood frozen, heedless of the fat yellow-green metastases sprouting as blood-soaked snot from the bronze of his musculature, amid the antiquated beauty of a cultic memorial fit for demolition, in cascades of filth shaken down as steam finally shot in bursts through the bottlenecks of pipes idle for eons to set in motion a forgotten epoch's driving rods…in a language that he owed to his status, that he'd learned at long last, touched and elevated by the coarsening enjoyment of all the ancient crimes of exploitation, he gasped out phrases of what seemed nineteenth-century caliber: the factory's situation is the symbol of the country's economic behavior, a form of progress commensurate with this patchwork of fiefdoms, but the victim is the class that, anticipating that so-called specter, that European specter, grins such a ghastly grin; before we're worn out and threadbare, let's flee across the sea again, *a proud ship*…oh, let us come to you, Africa of all unachieved things.

The stoker, diverted by a long, alarming coughing fit from a lapse into suchlike language, or at least rescued from an utterly inappropriate burst of mocking laughter, listened to the old foreman's soothing talk: Just one more round, and that'll be my last official act in this shack here. — When all the shot glasses had been refilled and everyone in the office was smoking: As you know, it's my duty to ask if you'd like to donate part of your bonus in solidarity, voluntarily of course, you know perfectly well what it's used for, I don't need to give you any lectures, the list right here in front of you, that's where you put your name down, and as you can see, all your colleagues' two percent obligations have already... — No, said the stoker, amazed at the awakening sound of his voice; the incisive, awful word had been uttered, and it echoed in the stillness of the office, a stillness against which the old foreman's voice barely stood out, seeming to talk on without paragraph breaks. — Yes, the old man went on, as you know, it's two percent a year, always paid without objections, my final duty here is to ask you, that's all, and if you do the math you'll see that that two percent hardly makes any difference at all. — The stoker uttered his words in an experimental form, as though aiming at a theatrical effect; they were words he'd rehearsed, he was detached from himself again, able to control them from outside. No, he repeated, I'm saying it loud and clear, no. This year there won't be any solidarity donation from me, because I believe we need to show solidarity toward ourselves first; I'm thinking of the working conditions in the Plant 6 boiler room. — If the stoker thought he could elicit a visible show of emotion from his former boss, he was mistaken. Of course, the foreman said, of course, I didn't build that boiler room, and I can't give you a new one, but of course the donation is voluntary, no one's forcing you. Besides, you don't have to pay it right away. — As he spoke, he pushed the list of donations, probably without thinking, back in front of the stoker, who, noticing nothing but that movement, declared in a loud voice: I said that I'm hereby *refusing* the donation, understand, *refusing* it, for the aforementioned reason I *decline* to make a donation. — Without looking at the old foreman, he sensed, from the cigarette smoke expelled a touch more emphatically from the man's nose, that he was smiling. At once the old man removed the list and hid it in a drawer. A pity really, he murmured, one column's left empty, but those measly twenty-six… — Two percent, the stoker said sharply. — Of course, two percent, the new foreman intervened in a conciliatory tone, albeit with a tremor he seemed unable to suppress, two percent, that's all. By the way, we're all aware that the bonuses came out smaller this year, but we ranked you at a higher level, is two percent too much to ask. — The stoker felt his concentration flagging: It's not about the size of the bonus… — Naturally, said the old foreman, naturally, you're the last one left, your ranking can't be changed now. — It's about the working conditions in that boiler room, a place that's the lowest level of all possible rankings, once you've descended to that level… — Naturally, the old foreman said calmly, if I weren't already standing with one foot in the grave…I'd say the aggravated conditions in Plant 6 have to be factored in more heavily when determining next year's bonuses. — It seems I'm being willfully misunderstood, the stoker persisted, I regard the Plant 6 boiler room as a kind of penal institution where you can't put a man for more than one winter if you don't want to lose him. I've been working there for seven years now, and I've got other pursuits. When I started there, I was promised it'd be for one heating season, no more, that's another thing that needs to be said, not in this office, but hopefully on a higher level. Before I quit my work in this operation I want to call attention to these things… — The stoker felt himself turning more and more unmistakably into a figure of his imagination, a literary figure whose lines slipped further and further into banality, phrases already devoid of value because they'd been calculated too far in advance, long since rendered obsolete by intervening, unexpectedly dramatic upheavals, so that now they diminished the issue at hand, cutting it down to a pathetic size. — Or does anyone have a different suggestion, does anyone see a way to abstain from this admittedly shabby form of protest, he said, already lacking all faith that his words would find a listener. — *Penal institution…protest*, the new foreman repeated, and right off the bat you're threatening to resign. You claim to be intellectually active, yet you ignore the fact that these donations may have rescued people from genuine penal institutions, you grew up in this country yet all you see is your boiler room; it's not hard to educate yourself about working conditions in developing countries that are just gaining their independence, do I have to give you a lecture… — The new foreman, still doubting the use of such exhortations, almost resolving upon a show of wrath, was turning away when the stoker interrupted him: That's exactly what I'm aware of, and that's why this question has to be discussed at a higher level. — At that exact point he felt that he'd already lost and conceded that round, but he continued all the same: My request is that if questions are asked, they should be answered in exactly the same spirit; it's my wish that further reflections on the statements I've made here should continue outside these four walls. — As you wish, the old foreman relented, if there's a single soul in this operation who cares to ask…due to dissatisfaction with his ranking, is that right…due to dissatisfaction with his post the stoker H. has…but I do hope this nonsense won't get around. — The stoker, having failed, even for a moment, to liberate himself from the lines of the figure whom he, *who'd grown up in this country*, was portraying, knew that his victory, determined by his own words, was actually a defeat, was a corrupting victory, the only one he could achieve in this country, a victory that, even if he instantly demanded paper and pen *to draft my resignation*, he'd only diminish; a resignation would merely have wheezed out something empty and unintelligible about the state of the Plant 6 boiler room, something that boiler room didn't even deserve, but it would have said nothing whatsoever about the state of his mind, which could no longer be brought into play here. — As though to finish things off with a touch of mockery, the new foreman said: What would you say if we told you there've been work brigades this year that pledged up to three percent, despite, sad to say, a dwindling payment fund. — From the point of view of my status, said the stoker, which I regard, which I'm forced to regard as a kind of slave status, it's irrelevant whether all the pros and cons have been considered, so long as it's possible to rise above the form you've grown into and gotten stuck in, above the form of the conflict possible within this status… — *Slave status*… said the new foreman, evidently seeing a chance to end the conversation by taking genuine offense, you call that a *slave status*, that's going way too far, if that's the way it is, we don't care to discuss it. Of course, this is something we'll be forced to reflect on further…but you can be sure: however much you may try to provoke it, there's no reason for us to advertise this sort of misconduct at a higher level.

The stoker, immediately shunted off into an insignificant supporting role, waited for a word that would cue his exit in the play performed by the actors in this office; the new director picked up a telephone receiver and dialed a number; reluctant to concede that the general silence was a call for him to leave, the stoker hunkered on the chair, slumping as low as though his hands were gripping the seat bottom, waiting for the phone conversation to begin, which took minutes; he was obviously trying to learn the reason for the phone call, and it was becoming embarrassing. Finally someone picked up, and the new director complained that the energy consumption data hadn't been relayed punctually at 7 AM. From the discussion that took place as the new foreman entered the missing figures onto a form, the stoker gathered that the person summoned to the phone was his colleague from Plant 6, who'd begun the early shift after he'd left that morning. The new director ended the conversation by saying that he regarded leniency toward fellow colleagues as a highly estimable quality: Even in cases like this, Colleague F., but we wouldn't appreciate your taking advantage of it. And your making a habit of coming late for the early shift. We might have to keep it in mind some day when calculating your wage. — Grinning attentively, the old foreman shook his head and looked at the stoker: So the next shift took over too late again today, it does seem like you guys in Plant 6 are having no end of trouble. — It was true, now the stoker recalled that at the end of his shift, after showering and changing, he'd waited in vain till past 6:30 for his relief; his colleague, who always picked up his bonus a day earlier, had announced that, however much money it turned out to be, he was going to go on a bender that night. With the fire in the boilers still holding out, the stoker had taken the risk and left; in the gray of dawn, filled with wind-driven snowflakes, he'd trooped to the derelict train station to catch one of the infrequently running passenger trains to M. With an uneasy feeling at having left the boilers under steam and unsupervised before the arrival of the next shift…what might happen if his colleague didn't turn up at all. It was in the hopes of seeing him disembark—he came from a town past M. and had to be on one of the trains whose lines converged here—that the stoker had positioned himself in the train car, nearly empty at that hour. Now he seemed able to recall the morning in every detail; he was sitting in the train, and the oncoming train from M. appeared in the distance as his got underway. As the two trains passed each other, greeting each other with toots, he scanned the row of windows in the cars shooting by on the next track and actually thought he glimpsed his colleague dozing by the window. But it could have been a figment of his imagination; when he got to the office, he'd have to reckon with the extremely awkward question of what he was doing there when they'd just gotten wind that the early shift hadn't arrived at Plant 6 yet. — The old foreman gave him a pitying smile: The next shift got there too late again. — And he clinked his empty brandy glass against the stoker's full one: Don't go forgetting that too, no hard feelings, we won't be seeing each other any time soon, I'm already a dead man here...don't forget to count your money, but do it outside... — The stoker, dismissed in conclusive, albeit conciliatory fashion, drained his glass in one swallow and left the office, swaying alarmingly; he felt that by recalling how he'd left his workplace on the train that morning, he'd managed to resolve at least one of that day's fateful entanglements; as he went, the secretary, who from the start of the argument had followed the scene silent and red-faced, but supporting the new foreman with repeated, unnoticed nods of her head, failed to respond to his goodbye, but that left him unmoved. — As soon as he heard his footsteps on the wooden boards of the shed's corridor and realized how shaky his footing was, it seemed to him, in a resurgence of awareness, that the entire factory was about to recede a vast distance behind him.

Outside, as the sun spread delicate vapors, brightening the slabs of the footpath between the still-unbulldozed, still-virginal-looking mounds of dirt on the grounds of what for years they'd been calling the *new* foundry; spring seemed to be coming, and the stoker felt a moment of liberation; the office, which had admitted no hint of the fine day it was turning out to be, lay behind him like the interior space of a dark past. He couldn't possibly go back to the boiler room; as soon as he got home, he'd draft his resignation…your last day of work will be the day I resign, that's what you've achieved, old foreman, he said. That old guard might be an ugly bunch of fossils, but the cadres of young managers now being installed all over the place were absolutely impossible to work with; you had to be crazy to expect anything from politically schooled careerists, bureaucrats from Day One; a new administration does not mean a new state… — There was still the two-week notice period, but he could handle that in his sleep; by then the winter would nearly be over and his departure would hardly hurt the factory. — He'd been sitting outside the factory entrance for a quarter of an hour on a bench dried by the sun, waiting for the bus to M.—not impatient yet, though the clock at the factory entrance showed ten after ten and the bus was supposed to leave at ten sharp—when one of the stokers from Plant 4, on the other side of the road some distance beyond the foundry, rode past on his bike. H. had known him for a long time and was surprised when the man didn't deign to glance at him, though he was sitting right there on the bench, the only person far and wide, impossible to overlook. He saw the cyclist take the turn of the path toward Shed 7 and asked himself whether that colleague had gotten word of his argument in the office, and what that word might have been. He began to suspect that the scandal was already common knowledge among his colleagues, the telephone made that easy, and that it was a conscious act on the other stoker's part to ride past without a greeting…that he was already an outcast, just minutes after his decision to quit.

However improbable it seemed, the new foreman had gotten a handle on the stokers the very first day he officially commenced his duties. They were split up among the separate boiler rooms, and there they remained, without a hint of flexibility; if one of them rebelled against the arrangement, he endangered the others who had better posts. It was a sophisticated strategy; for fear of having to replace a stoker promoted from Plant 6, no one would dare to underperform in front of the new foreman. It was impossible to remain in this operation; the sun that had greeted him on leaving the shed was not a light that would reveal him to himself in his true persona; that would take a sun that was absent here. As so often this morning, he saw himself as a completely thought-up, staged character, staged by a practically flawless system…describable only by external witnesses, now that he'd exited the factory he'd become an unperson named H. whose existence, he felt, all witnesses summoned would refuse to confirm, just as that cyclist could have ridden straight through his form without meeting any resistance.

He took the envelope out of his pocket to count the bonus. At the sight of the contents, he froze. Rather than the 650 marks he'd signed off on, the envelope contained *one thousand three hundred marks*, exactly twice the amount…a mistake. He counted it again, no doubt about it, 1,300 marks…he jumped up and raced back, and this time the policeman who'd been so suspicious this morning, but hadn't even looked at him when he left the factory, stopped him: What is it now, did you get your bonus or didn't you. — A mistake… The stoker shouted, I've got to go back right away, to the Energy Department, I forgot something… — What did you forget, the policeman drew out the words, I've had enough of this, do you have a pass. — I've got to go back…before the bus comes… — The policeman, sensing his advantage, showed his teeth triumphantly. — I'm going to hand in my resignation, the stoker blurted out. — Well, la-di-da, the operation can thank you for it, the policeman said, laughing openly in the stoker's face. At that moment the delayed bus arrived; the stoker walked over mechanically and got on through the doors that opened at once in front of him…exactly as he had that morning, he saw himself pale faced in the pane spattered from outside, and as though to utterly detach him from reality, the bus drove onward, hardly ever stopping, leaving him the sole passenger. — Bought off, he was a bought man, and the pocketed sum was no mistake; the envelope in his pocket contained double the bonus, precisely counted. All reality was annihilated, there would be no other reality until that evening, when he'd begun the night shift in his old boiler room, his writing utensils in front of him on the small table top roughly cleared of filth…the angrily darkening light would reveal them as the utensils of a nonexistent, vanished reality, or one that had never been; nothing on paper, however neatly written or printed, could have any claim to reality, he saw the sum of 650 marks entered next to his name in the bonus list, he saw that number distinctly, and next to it his signature. Once again he pulled the envelope out of his pocket and counted the money; on the enclosed card, printed with the state emblem and the initials of the operation, that expressed the management's thanks and congratulations, the dotted line left for the sum was filled with the number 650. Everything was in order; the stoker took seven 100-mark bills from the envelope and put them in his wallet, from which he removed a 50-mark bill to join the other six 100s in the envelope. A glance at the mirror over the driver's head reassured him that the driver's eyes were fixed straight ahead, on the road. Thus, all problems were banished from the world.

Are you finished for the day, the bus driver asked over the motor noise. — The stoker gave a start, but answered at once: No, this evening I start my second shift, in Plant 6. — Your second shift, yelled the bus driver. — Right, because we have to start Sunday evening already, by Monday morning the factory halls have to… — I know that, man, the driver yelled. And after a while: Today's Tuesday, what are these yarns you're spinning, don't you know what happened this morning… — And as the stoker racked his brains in silence: You were there, you said so yourself… Heinrich is dead, you've got to know who I mean, you knew the guy, your old porter from Plant 6. They found him this morning, but it was too late. — Dead… cried the stoker. — Run over, that's what they thought, early this morning, but I have a different theory…those Arabs, that rabble, backstabbers, scoundrels, all of them rabble, those savages, the driver ranted. — I don't know anything about it, said the stoker. — You idiot, yelled the driver, we were supposed to pick them up, from their party, weren't we. You said… You know perfectly well you said we had to pick those Arabs up in F., and then no one was there. — But Heinrich didn't even live in F. — You idiot, you're a total idiot, get out, man, won't you just get out, said the driver, stopping the bus and turning around, maybe his face has covered in tears, the stoker couldn't say, his neck straining forward, his gaze, like a snake's, fixed upon H. — The stoker fled the bus as though it were a room in which—inevitably, due purely to the darkness gathering there—he'd have been forced to commit some unknown crime. The bus station in M. was flooded by sunshine to which he was utterly impervious.

The alcohol put him to sleep at once, but he woke several times that day, his bed rumpled and sweat-drenched, one moist hand palpating his temples, feeling the thrum of a fever coming on. Until evening, however often he woke up, he fell back asleep in a state of strange exhaustion; in the intervals of waking, late in the day, as it grew dark again outside, as the street lamps switched on and filled the room with lunar radiance, he told himself he'd forgotten to draft his resignation. If the fever isn't gone after tomorrow's night shift, I'll take sick leave… resign and use my sick leave for the notice period, the thought calmed him so that he went back to sleep each time. — In a confused but unusually vivid dream that nearly made him late for his shift, he saw himself inside a pyramid, probably in its deepest chamber, amid stone sarcophagi in a hectic motile red light spewed by lamps covered in thick layers of soot; he saw himself working an endless row of boilers, ears filled with the incessant hiss of steam through countless pipes that passed overhead en route to the tip of the pyramid. He had an enormous, undwindling mound of coal to work with—even there the ends of sarcophagi jutted forth, broken from their pedestals, lying obstructively every which way—with unwaning strength he flung shovel after shovel of coal into the nearest boilers' flaring maws, the hissing in the steam pipes swelled, seeming to rise to the heights of the pyramid, and yet again insatiable flames lashed back from the boilers' mouths impossible to shut now. In the brief remaining intervals of respite he strained to hear footsteps above him, on the other side of the massive stone ceiling that capped this chamber; no doubt about it, up above there were footsteps everywhere, in all the rooms towering over him there was a pacing to and fro, but it was all drowned out by the noise of the steam. The question was when he would unearth the first corpse amid the shattered sarcophagi, it wouldn't be long before a yellow, wizened, aged face would stare up at him with broken eyes beneath his shovel blade, and over and over, thrusting the shovel into the coal, he'd meet the soft, tenacious resistance of a body; at last the fire settled into a steady raging, and he sank down trembling upon his dusty chair. — He still hadn't dared to draft his resignation yet. Or he wasn't capable of it; the text of his resignation would have the girth of a long book; he'd begun to write, setting down the endless chains of circumstances that text called for, but if he did manage to resolve everything and convey it in his text, to whom should he submit it. It was he himself that he handed the book to, the *stoker* had come to receive that resignation, with a lordly gesture he handed him, in exchange for the book, a large envelope in which coins and bills jostled, an exchange accompanied by his prodigious laughter, a laughter swallowed utterly by the steam pipes' deafening howls. He tried to recall his passage through a moonlit African landscape, under a sky dusted with sparkling stars, to descend into this underground room, but it was futile, the memory existed solely in the mind of the other man whom he saw walking away with the book, whom he saw climbing endless stairways, whose body, his spitting image, was still racked by laughter in the glow of the flames before vanishing into the darkness.